I0657765

ISBN: 978 1 7637532 1 1

First Edition.

This is a work of fiction, first written in 2015. Names, characters, places, and incidents are either the product of the author's imagination or used fictitiously. Any resemblance to actual events, locales, or persons, living or dead, is entirely coincidental.

Cover Design & Illustration by the author, P R Bird

Trigger warning: Explicit content, 18+ (NOT FOR YOUNGER READERS)

This book contains mature themes.

ECHOES OF THE SPALL

P R BIRD

FORWORD

Finnian Leif's life had been marked by tragedy, each event chipping away at his spirit until he became a mere shadow of himself. As a young pilot, he should have been soaring through the skies, revelling in the freedom of flight. Instead, the weight of his past pulled him down, tilting on the edge of alcoholism and self-destruction.

His demons began in his early adulthood when his closest friend, John, received a diagnosis of Acquired Immuno-deficiency Syndrome. Finnian could do nothing but watch helplessly as the cruel disease ravaged John's body, slowly extinguishing the light from his eyes. It was a wound that would never fully heal.

Then came the ill-fated night that changed everything. Under the influence of alcohol, Finnian made the reckless decision to get behind the wheel. His judgement clouded by insensibility, he collided with another vehicle, taking the lives of an innocent woman and her child. The guilt of unintentional manslaughter was a life sentence he could never escape.

As his PA-28 aircraft plummeted towards the ground and crashed in a desolate forest, Finnian was confronted once again with his demons. Stranded in the unforgiving wilderness, he had no choice but to come face-to-face with himself - the very thing he had been running from for so long.

As months pass without rescue, Finnian battled hunger and dehydration while also struggling with his mental state. Flashbacks of his past traumas tormented him, replaying the tragic events of that ominous night and the pain of losing someone close to him. He also couldn't escape the memories of those who had ridiculed him after the accident.

It wasn't until Finnian encountered a kermode bear that he found an unlikely ally. Though initially a terrifying presence, Finnian soon realised that the bear was a manifestation of his own inner turmoil - a physical representation of the trauma he had endured. This becomes evident when he finally realises that the bear does not want to kill him.

In a series of intense encounters, Finnian must confront his darkest thoughts and emotions. Each clash a reflection of the pain, guilt, and self-hatred he had carried for so long.

But as their ultimate showdown approached, Finnian understood that defeating the bear meant defeating himself - conquering the demons that had held him captive for too long. With newfound force, he faced his fears head-on and embraced the painful truths he had tried to bury. Like accepting the bear, he learnt to accept his past and move forward.

Finnian emerged victorious over both the bear and his inner struggles. The scars would remain, but he had achieved something even more significant - he had faced his trauma and come out on top. The wilderness had become his crucible, and he had emerged as a survivor, a warrior, and a man finally at peace with himself.

FINNIAN

As Finnian took his first tentative steps away from the prison, an unsettling chill crept up his spine. The world beyond the gates seemed too vast, too bright, too loud. Every car that passed made him flinch. Every glance from a stranger felt like an accusation.

He fumbled with the envelope marked "John," his fingers trembling. Inside was a crumpled piece of paper with an address scrawled in faded ink. It was his only lifeline in this alien landscape of freedom.

The sun beat down mercilessly as he walked, each step feeling heavier than the last. Shadows seemed to dance at the edges of his vision, taunting him with memories of the darkness he'd left behind. Freedom, he realised with growing dread, was its own kind of prison.

The road stretched endlessly before him, a ribbon of asphalt cutting through the desolate landscape. As twilight descended, shadows lengthened and twisted, taking on sinister shapes. Finnian's eyes darted nervously between the road and the rearview mirror, half-expecting to see flashing lights in pursuit.

A chill ran down his spine as he passed a weathered sign welcoming him to his hometown. The faded letters seemed to mock him, a grim reminder of all he'd left behind. The familiar streets now felt like a maze, each turn leading him deeper into a past he'd tried so hard to forget.

As he approached John's old house, a sense of dread settled in his stomach. The once-cheerful yellow paint was now peeling and grey, the windows dark and lifeless. Finnian parked across the street, his hands shaking as he reached for the envelope.

The door to his new life awaited, and with it, the shadow of his lost friend's memory. In that moment, he made a silent vow: to honour John's legacy, to rebuild, to find a semblance of peace in the chaotic aftermath of their shattered dreams.

Finnian stepped into the apartment, the door creaking ominously as it swung open. The place was sparse, the decor a mismatched collection of faded furniture and peeling wallpaper. A single overhead bulb cast a dim, yellowish light, struggling to illuminate the cramped space. It was more of a temporary shelter than a cozy home. For now, it would suffice.

He dropped his bag on the couch and looked around. A confined kitchen with old appliances, a squeaky wooden table, and a narrow hallway that he assumed led to the bedroom. The air was musty, carrying the scent of neglect. It was far from perfect, but after years behind bars, it was a step up.

Finnian pulled out his phone, thumbing through the notifications that had accumulated during his absence. One message caught his eye, a voicemail from his mum. He played it back, her voice trembling with emotion.

"Finnian, please call me when you can. Your father... well, you know how he is, but we need to talk."

He sighed, the weight of familial disappointment pressing down on him. The last thing he wanted was to hear about how he had let everyone down, especially from his father. The judgment, the unspoken anger, it was all too familiar. He tossed the phone onto the kitchen bench, deciding to ignore the voicemail for now.

He had a powerful impulse to run away as he felt trapped - the walls closing in around him. He grabbed his coat and headed out the door, making his way to the pub. As he walked, the cool evening air filled his lungs, a welcome change from the staleness of the apartment. The neon lights of the pub flickered in the distance, promising a brief respite from the chaos of his thoughts.

The pub wasn't quite as he remembered. Gone were the creaking floorboards and faded posters; in their place were polished wooden tables and freshly painted walls. Finnian barely recognised it. The staff had changed too, faces unfamiliar and the easy camaraderie of the past replaced with professional courtesy.

He smoothly seated himself on a stool at the bar. The leather beneath him was soft and new. A young woman with dark, curly hair and a warm smile approached. Her name tag read "Baree."

"What can I get you? "She asked, her tone piercing through the din of the busy pub.

Finnian requested a beer to calm his nerves. As she poured, he struck up a conversation.

"Been away for a while," he started, trying to make his tone sound casual. "Place looks different."

Baree nodded, handing him the drink. "Yeah, we had a renovation last year. Brought in new staff too. I've only been here a few months myself."

Finnian sipped his beer, the cold liquid a welcome distraction. "You wouldn't know if there are any jobs going around town, would you? Just moved here," he lied, the words slipping easily from his tongue. He thought it a more appropriate notion than explaining where he had truly been for the past 2 years.

Baree's eyes brightened with interest. "Actually, there might be. Depends on what you're looking for. What kind of work do you do?"

Finnian shrugged, keeping his answers vague. "A bit of everything, really. Just looking to get started."

Baree leaned on the counter, clearly curious. "Well, there's always work if you're willing to put in the effort. I've heard the hardware store is looking for help, and there's a new construction project starting up down by the old mill. Might be worth checking out."

Finnian nodded, grateful for the information. He continued to chat with Baree, finding her easy to talk to. There was something comforting about the normalcy of their conversation, a brief respite from the chaos that had defined his life.

As the night wore on, the pub filled with the sounds of laughter and clinking glasses. Finnian observed the familiar scene, experiencing a strange mix of nostalgia and detachment. He finished his drink and thanked Baree for her help, deciding it was time to head home.

Stepping out into the cool night air, Finnian felt a sense of unease. The past was always lurking, ready to pull him back into its grip. But for now, he had a new direction, a sliver of faith to hold on to. He walked back to his apartment, the envelope with John's name on it weighing heavily in his pocket. There were still many questions unanswered, many demons to face. But for the first time in a long while, Finnian felt an ounce of resolve.

Finnian walked up to the apartment door, hearing his phone ringing inside. He fumbled with the keys, and just as he opened the door, the ringing stopped. Inside, the small space exuded a more welcoming atmosphere now, a strange kind of solace in its simplicity. He checked his phone. Six missed calls from his mother. The sight of it made him sigh deeply.

He knew what awaited on the other end of the line; disappointment, frustration, the same conversation he'd been having for years. Finnian put the phone down on the kitchen bench, deciding he couldn't face it tonight.   Exhaustion washed over him, and he made his way to the bedroom. The bed creaked as he sat down, but it felt like a haven. As he laid down, the comfort of the mattress was almost overwhelming. A simple comfort he had missed. Sleep welcomed him.

The morning sun filtered through the curtains, casting a warm glow over the small apartment. Finnian groggily got out of bed. He brewed a pot of coffee, the rich aroma filling the kitchen. As he sat at the table, he picked up the envelope with John's name on it, turning it over in his hands. He considered opening it, curiosity gnawing at him. But the weight of the past was heavy, and he decided to wait.

Stuffing the envelope into his pocket, he grabbed his keys and headed out the door. The walk to the pub was brisk, the cool morning air invigorating. As he stepped inside, the pub was already bustling with the early preparations for the day. He found Baree in the back, rolling out empty kegs and replacing them with full ones.

"Morning," he called out, trying to sound more cheerful than his emotions indicated. Baree looked up, a smile spreading across her face.

"Hey, you're back! Need another drink already?" she teased.

Finnian chuckled, shaking his head. "Actually, I was hoping to find you. I don't really know anyone around here, and... well, I was wondering if you needed any help."

Baree paused, wiping her hands on her apron.

"Help, huh? Well, there's always plenty to do around here. I've got a list of jobs as long as my arm. You up for it?"

Finnian nodded, grateful for the distraction. "Absolutely. Just point me in the right direction."

She handed him a rag and pointed to the tables that needed wiping down. As they worked side by side, Finnian found himself opening up to Baree, sharing bits of his past and listening to her stories about life in the town. The work was not so challenging, yet it was satisfying to be helpful and establish a connection with someone.

With each task, Finnian felt a little more grounded, a little more at home. And as the day progressed, he came to the realisation that perhaps this place offered the potential for fresh starts.

As they worked through the list of bar tasks, Baree caught Finnian glancing at her with a small smile. She raised an eyebrow and smirked. "You know, if you're trying to pick me up, there are easier ways."

Finnian laughed, shaking his head. "No, nothing like that. I just... appreciate the company. It's been a while since I've had a decent conversation with someone. Female company is a breath of fresh air."

Baree paused; curiosity piqued. "What do you mean? Where have you been?"

He hesitated, not ready to divulge the full truth. "Let's just say I've been away for a bit. Had some time to reflect." She gave him a knowing look.

Finnian's smile faded, replaced by a shadow of regret. "It involved a DUI.

It's not like I murdered someone."

"That is not what I was thinking at all," she laughed.

16

"It is literally the first thing that comes to mind when people say that they've been in prison." Finnian scoffed playfully.

Baree could see a flicker of something in his eyes, but didn't push to query what it may be. Instead, she smiled warmly. "Alright, fair enough. How about we grab some lunch? We've finished all the bar jobs for now, and you look like you could use a proper meal."

Finnian's stomach growled at the suggestion, and he realised how hungry he was. "Lunch sounds great. Lead the way."

Baree stretched and wiped her hands on her apron. "You know, I'm actually pretty tired of eating at the pub every day. How about we grab a burger from that little stand down the road and take it to the jetty? It's a nice spot to sit and chat."

Finnian smiled, appreciating the offer. "Sounds perfect."

They ordered their burgers and made their way to the jetty, the wooden planks creaking softly under their feet as they sat down. The sun glinted off the water, casting shimmering reflections.

As they unwrapped their food, the conversation flowed easily. Finnian found himself opening up to Baree about life, his time in prison, and his plans for a fresh start. Baree shared stories of her own, from working at the pub to her dreams of travelling.

The peaceful setting and the warm sun made it easy to forget the weight of the past for a while. They finished their burgers and sat in comfortable silence, watching the water lap against the shore.

"Thanks, Baree," Finnian said, breaking the silence. "It's been a long time since I've felt this... normal."

She smiled, nudging him playfully. "Everyone deserves a chance to start over."

The next morning, Finnian woke up to the soft light streaming through the curtains. He made a cup of coffee, savouring the warmth as he pondered his plans for the day. He didn't want to seem too clingy to Baree, so he decided to finally open the envelope John had left him.

Inside, he found a set of keys and a note with an address a few kilometres out of town. Curious, he grabbed his own keys and headed out. The drive was peaceful, the rural landscape slipping by as he followed the directions. He soon arrived at an airplane bunker tucked away from the main road.

With a mixture of apprehension and excitement, Finnian unlocked the door. Inside, the smell of aviation gas brought back a flood of memories. There, gleaming under the dim lights, was a small plane, a Piper Archer PA-28, similar to the one he used to own before the accident. John had left this for him, a final gift, knowing how much flying meant to him.

Finnian climbed into the cockpit, the familiar controls under his fingertips. The sleek, leather-bound steering wheel, the array of dials and gauges, all felt like an extension of himself. The plane's fuselage glinted under the soft glow of the bunker lights; every inch meticulously maintained.

As he started the engine, the hum resonated with memories of the countless hours he'd spent in the skies. He remembered taking John flying when he was sick, how those moments of soaring above the earth had brought a rare smile to his friend's face. The freedom of the open sky had been an escape for both of them, a brief reprieve from the reality of John's illness. Those flights had become more than just a pastime; they were a sanctuary, a place where John could forget about his pain, if only for a little while.

Finnian reached for his phone, fingers trembling slightly as he composed a text to Baree.

"Hey Baree, what are your plans for the weekend?"

After hitting send and leaning back in the pilot's seat, a strange mix of faith and anticipation enveloped him. The plane's gentle hum was like a heartbeat, grounding him as he waited for her reply.

His mind wandered back to those days with John, the wind rushing past, the laughter and quiet moments shared thousands of feet above the earth. He could almost hear John's voice, his laughter, and see the joy in his eyes as they soared through the clouds. The plane was more than just a machine; it was a vessel of memories, a symbol of their bond.

Finnian cut off the engine and climbed out of the plane, his boots hitting the tarmac with a resolute thud. The sun dipped low, casting long shadows across the airfield. Just as he slammed the door shut, an older woman approached. It was Igrit, John's mother. She was covered in grease, her hair a messy tangle that spoke of countless hours spent in the hangar.

Finnian met her with a hug that was more than a greeting; it was a bridge over the years of absence. Igrit's voice was thick with emotion as she whispered, "I've missed you, Finnian. Not a day has gone by since John's funeral…" Her words trailed off, leaving the air heavy with unspoken grief.

"I'm sorry I couldn't stay for the wake," Finnian murmured, his voice barely audible over the hum of the cooling engine.

Igrit pulled back slightly, her eyes searching his. "I always hoped you'd come back for the plane. John never got to earn his flying license. He grew too sick… too fast. But do you remember that time you took him up? You let him take the controls…" Her voice broke, and for a moment, they were both lost in the memory.

Finnian nodded, a faint smile tugging at the corners of his mouth. "He was a natural. Even then, I knew he had the spirit for it."

Igrit's hand, rough and calloused, closed around his. "He looked up to you, you know." The weight of her words settled on Finnian's shoulders, a bittersweet reminder of the bond they all shared. The plane stood as a silent witness to dreams unfulfilled and the enduring ties of family.

She glanced at the plane and then back at Finnian. "Are you taking it up today?"

Finnian shook his head. "No, I'm headed to town to check or renew my flying license. My parents moved to a little remote town up near Sitka about six months ago. I plan on flying up there for the weekend."

"Oh, how lovely. Your mother and I don't talk much at all these days. Wish her well for me, please."

Finnian nodded softly with a smile, "How's Marty doing?"

"Marty is struggling, Finn," Igrit spoke in a sombre voice, "Some days he doesn't even get out of bed. But…we are going away for a while. Taking a trip.

There are too many memories here of John."

"A trip? That would be nice. How long are you away for?"

"Six months at the latest. See how we go, I suppose. His knees play up on him a bit."

Finnian gave a knowing nod.

"Let's catch up properly when you're back. Enjoy your time away. Some fresh air ought to do you both good." Igrit nodded, understanding.

She walked him out to his car, their footsteps crunching softly on the gravel. At the car, she hugged him tightly, reluctant to let go. "Oh, if you take the plane out at all while we're gone, close up the hanger, will you? Damn swallows poop all over everything in there".

"Sure thing", he breathed through a grin.

"Take care, Finnian."

He returned the embrace. "You too, Igrit."

As he drove away, the plane and the woman who held onto so many dreams grew smaller in the rearview mirror, yet their presence loomed large in his heart.

JOHN

The hospital had become a prison to John, its barren walls and the constant drone of machines a bleak reminder of his impending fate. The disease had ravaged his body, each day bringing new pain and challenges. Despite it all, he clung to the moments of stillness, reminiscing about the days before his illness consumed him entirely. He treasured the visits from Finnian, their conversations a brief reprieve from the harsh reality of the hospital. They spoke of everything and nothing, finding solace in each other's presence.

As his condition worsened, John felt a sense of resignation settle over him. He made the decision to face each day with bravery, drawing strength from the love and support surrounding him. The doctors and nurses became like family, their kindness a lifeline in his darkest moments. John formed friendships with other patients, their shared struggles to create bonds that went beyond words. In the quiet hours of the night, he poured out his heart in letters, expressing emotions he struggled to articulate aloud. These letters brought him comfort, a way to make sense of the overwhelming whirlwind of feelings.

But amidst all this resilience, there were also moments of deep sorrow and regret. The memory of the party where he was mocked and ridiculed haunted him, a cruel reminder of ignorance and hatred. Yet even as bitterness threatened to consume him, John refused to give in. Instead, he found purpose in small acts of kindness, whether it was offering a reassuring smile to a struggling patient or expressing gratitude towards the hospital staff. In facing his mortality, John discovered an inner strength to live each day with dignity.

He had scrawled a note at the top of his notepad 'Finnian's plane.'

FINNIAN

Finnian pulled into the pub, a small, cozy place with a warm atmosphere, where time seemed to slow down. He stepped inside, the familiar scents of aged wood and beer greeting him. Sliding into a booth, he glanced around, hoping to catch sight of Baree. But she wasn't there.

The absence tugged at him, a mix of disappointment. He flagged down the bar attendant, who shook his head.

"Sorry mate, Baree isn't working today."

Finnian, trying to mask his disappointment, asked, "Do you know where I can find her?"

The attendant eyed him suspiciously. "How do you know her? I haven't seen your face around before."

Finnian gave a friendly smile, hoping to ease the tension. "I'm just a friend."

The attendant seemed unconvinced, but after a moment of consideration, he nodded. "Alright, just a friend. But I don't know where she is. Sorry."

Finnian nodded, appreciating the effort. He walked back to a quiet corner of the bar, pulled out his phone, and saw a new message from Baree. His heart skipped a beat as he read: "Out of town, back tonight. Catch up?"

Finnian typed back quickly, "Definitely. Let me know when you're back." He hit send and felt a flicker of excitement.

Later that night, Finnian's phone buzzed with a new message from Baree: "At the club. Join us?" He hesitated for a moment before deciding to go. The club was a cacophony of lights and sounds, the bass thumping in his chest as he stepped inside. He weaved through the crowd, a sense of unease creeping up his spine. The thick air smelled of sweat and alcohol; a wave of panic washed over him.

He spotted Baree among a lively group of her girlfriends, all laughing and drinking. Her face lit up when she saw him, her smile a beacon in the chaos. She waved him over.

"Hey, face like Eve Hewson," called Finnian

Baree turned toward him; a playful frown strewn across her face.

"Hey, face like…Tanner Buch…anan," returning the jest.

27

"Tanner Buchanan? I was thinking more like Henry Cavill, but excuse me" Finnian laughed, stepping back with his hands raised cooly in surrender. He made his way to them, trying to steady his breathing as the atmosphere changed.

"Sorry. I tend to blurt out strange things when I'm uncomfortable."

Baree nodded, pressing her lips into a thin line in understanding.

She noticed his discomfort and gave him a concerned look. "Do you want to get out of here?"

"Please?"

Baree caught a flicker of something in his eyes, pain, regret, or perhaps both. She excused herself from the group and followed him outside into the cool night air. They walked along the quiet street, the distant thrum of the club fading behind them.

Finnian hesitated, his steps slowing. He took a deep breath, the words heavy on his tongue. "I'm not comfortable in situations like that," he admitted, his voice low but steady. "With all the...people... and the alcohol. I've been there before, and I would much rather not go back."

Baree gazed at him with a surprising level of understanding. "Our pasts don't define who we are."

Finnian sensed a weight lift off his shoulders, the night air suddenly seeming less heavy.

As they walked, Baree's curiosity got the better of her. "Finnian, what happened in the accident?" she asked gently, her voice a whisper.

Finnian's expression darkened, a shadow passing over his features. He stopped walking, his gaze fixed on a distant, unseen point. "I'm not ready to talk about it," he said, his voice thick with emotion. The weight of the unspoken words hung between them.

Baree nodded, her understanding deep and unwavering. She reached out and rubbed his shoulder, a simple gesture that carried with it a world of comfort. They continued their walk in silence.

The pier stretched out before them, a bridge between land and sea. They reached the end and sat down, the wood cool and solid beneath them. The marina was a canvas of gentle motion and light, boats bobbing on the water, their lights casting flickering reflections that danced on the surface.

Finnian's mind drifted back to the accident; the memories sharp. After experiencing the familiar ache of guilt and regret, the emotions within him swirled like a storm. Beside Baree, a sense of ease washed over him. Her mere presence comforted him; a balm to his wounded soul, her silent companionship a reminder that he was not alone.

The quiet of the night wrapped around them, the soft lapping of the waves a soothing backdrop to their shared silence. They sat there for a long time, watching the boats sway in the water.

The night sky exploded with fireworks, set off by exuberant partiers on a nearby boat. The display filled the air with vibrant colours and deafening booms, each burst of light reflecting off the calm waters of the marina. Baree turned to Finnian; her eyes wide with wonder. The intensity of the fireworks mirrored the growing tension between them, each bang and pop sending vibrations through their chests.

Amid the dazzling light show, emotions swelled and mingled. Thick suspense hung in the air, filled with unspoken words and shared feelings. Finnian reached for Baree's hand, their fingers intertwining.

As the grand finale lit up the sky, a cascade of colours falling like a shower of stars, Baree and Finnian leaned towards each other. In that suspended instant, only the two of them existed.

Their lips met, gentle at first but growing more passionate as they lost themselves in each other. Baree pulled away abruptly. Finnian searched her eyes, confusion enveloping him. "I'm sorry," she started, "I just wasn't expecting that so soon."

Finnian continued to peer into her eyes, a small smile forming on his lips. Her admission suggested that their budding emotions were mutual. In that moment, it was all he needed to know.

BAREE

As the evening sun cast its warm glow over Finnian's face, Baree sat across from him, listening intently to his words. She was struck by the genuine kindness and thoughtfulness in which he spoke, a rare quality she had not encountered before. Despite only knowing each other for two days, Baree felt a deep connection with Finnian that resonated within her.

He was unlike her ex-husband, Justin, in every way. Instead of harshness and dismissiveness, Finnian exuded gentleness and attentiveness. He cared about important things - people, the world - and it showed in everything he did. As Baree watched him talk, she felt a warmth stirring in her chest and belly, a feeling she had never experienced before, even with Justin.

Finnian continued to share his thoughts and dreams, his eyes lighting up as he spoke with honesty and vulnerability. His openness captivated Baree, drawn to him like a magnet. The conversation flowed effortlessly between them, building a sturdy bridge of connection with each passing moment.

Talking to Finnian was easy; there were no walls or pretences between them. They found succour in each other's company, their souls connecting on a deeper level. Baree marvelled at the simplicity of it all, at how perfectly they seemed to fit together. In Finnian, she saw more than just a companion; she saw a potential partner who truly understood her.

As the evening progressed, Baree's feelings for Finnian grew stronger. She knew this was something special and needed to hold on to it. The warmth in her chest spread, filling her with optimism and possibility. For the first time in a long while, she allowed herself to believe that true love and connection were possible.

Baree grew up in a small coastal town, perpetually dreaming of exploring beyond the horizons she could view from her bedroom window. Her father was a fisherman, and her mother ran a quaint bookstore brimming with tales of adventure and mystery. As a child, she would spend hours in the shop, losing herself in the pages of books, imagining herself in far-off lands.

Her parents' work ethic and passion for simple things shaped her into a grounded, yet curious individual. Despite her courageous spirit, she stayed close to home to help with the family business after her father passed away unexpectedly. The loss hit her profoundly, but it also strengthened her resolve to cherish and support those she loved.

Baree's teenage years were filled with balancing school, helping her mother, and finding solace in music. She learned to play the guitar, her father's old instrument, and began performing at local venues. Her music became an outlet for her emotions, a way to connect with others and process her grief.

In her early twenties, Baree saved up enough to travel. She visited various countries, soaking in different cultures, and learning more about herself in the process. Each place she visited added to her character, leading to her becoming more empathetic and wiser.

Throughout her travels, Baree developed a profound love for nature. She found peace in hiking through dense forests, camping under starlit skies, and diving into the depths of the ocean. Her escapades in nature became a source of inspiration for her music and her life philosophy, embracing simplicity, harmony, and the beauty of the natural world.

Eventually, Baree returned to her hometown, bringing with her a wealth of experiences and a renewed appreciation for home. She took up a job at a local bar to stay connected with the community and continued to play music; her performances now infused with the stories and sounds of her travels and her deep connection to nature.

Baree also carried the scars of a brief but tumultuous marriage. She had married young, hoping to build a life with someone she thought she knew. But her partner turned out to be abusive, and after six harrowing months, she found the strength to leave. The experience left her wary but resilient, resolute to never let anyone dim her spirit again.

Baree's reflections were like unwelcome intruders, slipping into her mind when she least expected it. Her flashbacks were vivid, each one a painful reminder of the past she was trying to leave behind. She could still feel the sting of his words, the way they cut through her just like a knife. The apprehension that had once gripped her heart resurfaced in waves, rendering it hard to breathe.

She remembered the way he would look at her, his eyes brimming with a cold, calculating anger. The way he would speak, each word laced with venom. The manner in which he would grab her arm, his grip tight and unyielding, leaving bruises that took weeks to fade. The way in which he would apologise afterward, his voice soft and pleading, promising that it would never happen again. But it always did.

The flashbacks were relentless, dragging her back to those moments of terror and helplessness. She could hear his voice, feel his touch, see his face. It was as if he was still there, haunting her with every step. She tried to push the memories away, to focus on the present, but they clung to her as a shadow, always lurking just out of sight.

Baree understood she had to face these memories, to confront the pain and terror that they brought. She had to remind herself that she was no longer that scared, helpless girl. She was stronger now, braver. She had survived, and she would continue to survive. The past was a part of her, but it did not define her.

She was adamant about creating a future free from the shadows of her past.

FINNIAN

Finnian stared at his phone, the missed call from his mother glaring back at him. He knew he should return her call, she'd probably worry if he didn't. Besides, with Baree out of town for the weekend, his options for company were dwindling. He had no desire to face the awkward conversations with friends who were still blissfully unaware of his time in prison or who would inevitably bring up the accident.

With a sigh, he dialled her number. The phone barely rang before she picked up, her voice warm and filled with that familiar maternal concern. "Finnian, darling! I was getting worried. Everything alright?"

He forced a smile, even though she couldn't see it. "Hey Mum, yeah, everything's fine. Just been busy, you know how it is."

"Busy? Well, I hope you're taking care of yourself. You sound tired."

He hesitated, his mind racing for the right words. "Actually, I was thinking of coming up to see you and Dad this weekend. I thought it might be nice to spend some time together since…well…. I'm out."

There was a pause on the other end, and he could almost hear her smiling.   "Oh, Finnian, that would be wonderful! We have missed you. And I could use some help with the garden, if you're up for it."

A small chuckle escaped him as he considered the idea of getting his hands dirty in the garden. Somehow, it felt like a comforting thought. "Yes, that sounds nice. It'll be good to catch up and lend a hand."

There was a moment of quiet on the phone, but he could almost feel her smiling on the other end.

"Looking forward to it," he replied, feeling some weight lift from his shoulders. Maybe spending a weekend with his parents would help him ease back into society or what passed for normalcy.

"We'll see you soon then. Travel safely, my boy," his mother's voice said, filled with emotions.

Finnian felt a mix of emotions as he arrived at his parents' home. His mother greeted him warmly with a tight hug, her eyes shining with unspoken relief.

"It's great to have you home, Finnian," she whispered, holding on for a bit longer as if shielding him from any worries. Meanwhile, his father stood a couple of steps back with his arms crossed.

"Good to see you, son," he said with a cool tone and distant demeanour. The chill in his voice was vast and contrasted sharply with his mother's warmth. John had always been a point of contention between them, and time had only made the rift grow wider.

The dinner table was a quiet affair. His father mostly kept to himself, the occasional grunt or nod his only contributions to the conversation. His mother filled the silence with tales of the garden, the latest news from town, anything to keep the atmosphere light.

After dinner, Finnian found himself alone with his mother in the cozy living room. She looked at him with a mix of love and concern. "How are you really, Finnian?" she asked softly, not prying, but genuinely wanting to know.

He paused, the weight of her question settling over him.

"I'm… managing. I miss him," he replied, looking away for a moment. The silence stretched between them, a comfortable one, filled with the unspoken understanding only a mother could provide.

"I didn't get to say goodbye. I was put away, and he was just gone. They wouldn't even allow me to attend the wake."

His mother squeezed his hand, at a loss for words. It's the only way she knew how to offer comfort.

Finnian sat across from his mother at the coffee table, the quiet hum of the house a stark contrast to the heaviness that hung in the air. The comforting smell of freshly brewed tea did little to ease the weight of their conversation.

"I miss John too. But I am also just so relieved that you're out."

"I know," he sighed, "It still feels like a miracle, Mum. That man, the pizza delivery guy, coming forward after all this time. It's hard to believe." His voice shook with emotion as he spoke.

His mother's eyes reflected the sorrow that had lingered for years. "I can't imagine how it must feel for you, Finnian. But thank goodness he finally came forward. I always knew you were innocent."

Finnian looked down at his hands, his grip tightening on his cup. "But I wasn't, mum. I'm not innocent. I was drinking. I probably would have had better control over the car if I hadn't been drinking that much."

She reached out and grasped his hand; "You should never have had to endure that burden. What happened was a tragedy, but I'm grateful that justice has been served."

Their gazes met and Finnian's pain was clear in his eyes. "It doesn't change what happened though... those two lives lost will never come back."

His mother's hand tightened around his. "But at least now you know the truth. And you have a chance to rebuild your life, to find peace and honour their memory."

He nodded, the burden of the past bearing down on him. Love and sympathy filled her smile. In that moment, he felt a mix of closure and grief wash over him. It was a new beginning, but one tinged with sadness and regret. The past may have shaped him, but he was determined to not let it define his future.

After what felt like an eternity, he took a deep breath and shared a piece of information he had told no one yet. An uplifting element to improve the atmosphere.

"I met someone, Mum," he said, his voice barely above a whisper.

Her eyes lit up, a gentle smile playing on her lips. "That's wonderful,

Finnian. Do you want to tell me about them?"

He shook his head slightly. "Not yet. But maybe someday."

His mother nodded, her smile never fading.

The visit to his mother brimmed with warmth and reminiscence, providing a much-needed respite for both of them. But as Finnian prepped the plane for his return journey, he couldn't ignore the ominous clouds gathering on the horizon.

His mother watched him with worried eyes.

"Are you sure it's safe to fly, Finnian?" she asked, her voice tinged with anxiety.

Finnian gave her a reassuring smile, though his own stomach knotted at the sight of the darkening sky. "It's fine, Mum. The forecast says the rain's patchy, nothing serious. I'll be home before you know it."

As Finnian took off, the familiar hum of the engine filled the cockpit. The first leg of the journey was uneventful, the patchy rain as expected. But soon, the clouds thickened, turning the sky into a foreboding canvas of grey.

Finnian's hands tightened around the yoke as he navigated his small plane through the skies, the vast expanse of a rainforest stretching out beneath him. The dense green canopy, interspersed with winding rivers and rugged mountains, was a breathtaking sight. The hum of the engine was a comforting sound, a steady rhythm that calmed his nerves. He glanced at the instruments, ensuring everything was in order, then reached for the radio to establish communication with the tower.

"Sitka Tower, this is November One-Niner-Three-Echo. Requesting permission to ascend to 10,000 feet, over."

The radio crackled for a moment before a clear voice responded. "November One-Niner-Three-Echo, this is Sitka Tower. Permission granted.
Maintain heading of two-seven-zero, over."

"Copy that, Sitka Tower. Ascending to 10,000 feet. Heading two-seven zero. November One-Niner-Three-Echo, out."

Finnian adjusted the controls, feeling the plane respond smoothly as it climbed to the new altitude. The view from the cockpit was even more spectacular from this height, the vastness of the rainforest stretching to the horizon. The sunlight glinted off the surface of the rivers below, creating a patchwork of light and shadow.

"Seattle Centre, this is November One-Niner-Three-Echo. Checking in at 10,000 feet. Heading two-seven-zero, over."

The response came promptly. "November One-Niner-Three-Echo, this is Seattle Centre. You're on course. Be advised, weather reports indicate potential storm activity ahead. Proceed with caution, over."

He glanced at the instruments. Everything seemed normal, yet his grip on the yoke tightened.

Finnian felt a knot of anxiety tighten in his stomach. He had checked the weather before take-off, but conditions could change rapidly in this region. "Copy that, Seattle Centre.

Proceeding with caution. November One-Niner-Three-Echo, out."

He kept a close eye on the instruments, scanning the horizon for any signs of the approaching storm. The sky ahead seemed to darken slightly, and he could see clouds gathering in the distance. The radio crackled to life again.

The first drops of rain spattered against the windscreen, followed by a sudden gust of wind that rocked the plane. Finnian's heart raced, but he kept his course, confident in his ability to navigate the storm. The memory of his mother's worried eyes lingered in his mind, driving him forward with a steely perseverance.

"November One-Niner-Three-Echo, this is Seattle Centre. Radar shows a significant storm cell developing. Advise you to alter course to avoid the worst of it. Over."

Finnian's heart pounded. He knew that navigating a storm in a small plane was risky, but he had to stay calm.

"Seattle Centre, this is November One-NinerThree-Echo. Acknowledged. Altering course to three-zero-zero. Over."

"Copy that, November One-Niner-Three-Echo. Stay safe out there. Seattle Centre, out."

Finnian adjusted the heading, feeling the plane respond to the alternative course. The clouds were closing in, and he could feel the first drops of rain spatter against the windshield. The hum of the engine was now joined by the rhythmic patter of the rain, creating a symphony of sound inside the cockpit.

The storm hit suddenly; strong winds and heavy rain buffeted the plane. Visibility dropped to almost nothing, and Finnian's hands gripped the yoke tightly as he fought to maintain control. The turbulence was fierce, shaking the small aircraft with alarming intensity.

"Seattle Centre, this is November One-Niner-Three-Echo. Encountering severe turbulence. Requesting guidance, over."

The storm was not what he expected. He felt the aircraft lurch; the controls becoming increasingly unresponsive. Through the rain-streaked glass, he could barely make out the landscape below.

The radio crackled, but the response was faint, almost drowned out by the noise of the storm. "November One-Niner-Three-Echo, maintain current heading.

We're tracking you, over."

Finnian nodded to himself, his focus entirely on keeping the plane steady. The storm raged on, but he knew he had to trust in his skills and the communication with the tower. The rainforest below was a dense, untamed expanse, and he had to navigate through this chaos to find safety.

Suddenly, a violent gust of wind rocked the plane, knocking it off course. Finnian fought to regain control, but the storm's fury was relentless. The instruments were going haywire, the altimeter spinning wildly as the plane lost altitude.

It was then he realised the true peril of underestimating nature's unpredictability, a peril that would soon plunge him into an ordeal he wasn't sure he could survive. The plane banked sharply to the left, and Finnian fought to level it out. Sweat beaded on his forehead as he pulled back on the yoke, but the aircraft seemed to have a mind of its own.

"Mayday, mayday, this is November One-Niner-Three-Echo. I've lost
control."

The horizon tilted; the sky was a dizzying reel of dark grey, and white flashes of lightning. Turbulence rocked the plane, and Finnian felt the sickening drop in altitude as a downdraft caught the aircraft. His hands trembled as he fought against the force of the storm, the turbulence jolting through his body like electric shocks. The weightlessness in his stomach made him feel like he was floating, yet the pressure against his chest reminded him of the imminent threat.

The air inside the cockpit grew stale and stifling; suffocating him as he struggled to regain control.

"Mayday, mayday, this is November One-Niner-Three-Echo. I've lost control."

As the plane continued to be buffeted by the turbulence, Finnian's heart raced, pounding against his ribcage as adrenaline flooded his system. His heart momentarily faltered as the plane began a downward spiral more rancorous than before. The disarray of the once-calm sky, now a swirling vortex sending him to his death.

Despite his efforts to remain calm, his body betrayed him, trembling with a combination of fear and exertion.

"Mayday, mayday."

The unresponsive controls and the loss of communication only added to Finnian's sense of helplessness.

He could feel the strain in his muscles as he fought against the erratic movements of the aircraft.

Finnian's stomach lurches as the plane banks sharply, his insides churning with a sickening mix of fear and adrenaline. The once stable horizon now tilts at alarming angles, disorienting Finnian and making it impossible to gauge the plane's trajectory.

"Mayday, mayday, this is November One-Niner-Three-Echo! I'm going down!" Finnian screams into the radio, his voice trembling with panic. But all he receives in response is a deafening wall of static, drowning out any promise for rescue. The aircraft spun faster and faster, gaining speed as it plummeted toward the earth. Unease overcame Finnian as his line of sight caught a forest of trees looming toward him too fast for him to comprehend, too fast to anticipate the moment of impact. Suddenly, he slipped unconscious; the thought was too much to process.

Silence.

THE BEAR

The bear rummaged for food in the pouring rain, its coat glistening with water droplets as it foraged. Suddenly, a deafening roar pierced through the stormy sky. The bear looked up to see a metallic bird hurtling towards the earth. The plane left a trail of smoke behind as it careened toward the ground, its descent out of control and swift. The impact was explosive, shaking the trees and causing birds to scatter frantically.

The bear stood still for a moment, the crash's echoes still ringing through the forest. Rain continued to fall heavily, creating a symphony of drips on leaves and soil. An inner conflict tugged at the bear's instincts - both curiosity and caution urging it to move closer towards the disturbance. As it approached cautiously, drawn by the strange smell of gas and metal intermingled with the earthy scent of the rain-soaked forest.

As the bear neared the crash site, all its senses were on high alert. The remains of the plane lay scattered, an unfamiliar intrusion in the peaceful landscape. Rain sizzled as it hit hot surfaces of the aircraft, sending wispy tendrils of steam into the air. From a safe distance, the bear watched with dark reflective eyes, taking in the chaos and destruction before it. The bear's keen eyes spotted the man inside, slumped over and unconscious.

The bear circled the wreckage, its massive paws crunching on broken branches and debris. It approached the window, peering inside. The man was still, his face pale and bloodied. The bear's instincts kicked in, it needed to act. With powerful thrusts, the bear began pushing on the window glass, its paws thudding against the surface. The glass popped under the immense pressure, cracks veining with each impact. The bear's growls filled the air, a mix of urgency and perseverance.

Inside the plane, Finnian stirred. The noise and vibrations pulled him from the depths of unconsciousness. His eyes fluttered open, and he was met with the sight of the bear's colossal form looming outside the window. Panic surged through him, his heart pounding in his chest.

The bear's eyes met his, and for a moment, Finnian was paralysed with fear.

FINNIAN

Finnian staggered out of the party, his heart pounding and his thoughts racing. The rain was coming down in sheets, mingling with the tears he refused to shed. The shouts and jeers of the boys still echoed in his ears, their hateful words a relentless barrage on his psyche.

He fumbled with his car keys, his hands shaking as he finally unlocked the door. Sliding into the driver's seat, he took a deep breath, trying to steady himself. The car was being pummelled by the fierce storm, with rain and hail coming down hard. Visibility was almost non-existent, but he had to get away. Away from the party, away from the memories; the torment.

The road was slick and treacherous, the windshield wipers struggling to keep up with the deluge. Finnian's knuckles were white as he gripped the steering wheel, his eyes straining to see through the torrent. He barely noticed the pizza delivery guy on his push bike until it was too late.

The cyclist swerved into the road, and Finnian's reflexes awoken. To avoid a crash, he pivoted the wheel, causing the car to skid uncontrollably. The next few moments were a blur of screeching tires, shattering glass, and the sickening crunch of metal.

Finnian's car collided with another vehicle, a mother and her young son, their faces a flash of terror before the impact sent both cars careening off the road and into the lake. The water was glacial, filling the car with alarming speed. Finnian struggled to unbuckle his seatbelt, panic rising as the water filled the vehicle. He pounded on the window, the surface barely yielding under his desperate fists.

A murky figure materialised through the water's darkness. A person, drawn by the crash, was swimming frantically towards him. The stranger got to the car and started aggressively smashing the window with a tyre iron, displaying a sense of urgency and resolve.

Finnian's vision blurred as the water rose to his neck. He could see the figure's strained expression; the sheer effort etched into their features. A web of cracks veined down the centre of the glass, giving way to spurts of water as the screen threatened to give way at any moment.

A thunderous pounding jolted him from his dream. Pain radiated through his body as he blinked into consciousness. His head throbbed; his limbs felt leaden. The cockpit was a tomb of twisted metal and shattered glass, the once sleek machine now a crumpled wreck. He tried to move, but his vision swam with darkness. Finnian's heart raced as he turned to the source of the pounding. The aircraft's hood buckled under the weight of the giant grey bear standing on it. The animal's fur was damp from the rain.

The glass shattered, sending shards cascading inside the cockpit. Finnian shielded his face with an arm, his heart pounding as the bear's form loomed through the newly created opening. The air was thick with tension, every second stretching into an eternity.

For a moment, Finnian remained frozen, unsure of the bear's intentions. The creature's sheer size and power were overwhelming, a force of nature right before him. But instead of attacking, the bear seemed to study him, its gaze intense and probing.

With a low, rumbling growl, the bear attempted to climb into the wreckage, its movements deliberate and controlled.

Finnian's instincts screamed at him to run, but his body remained rooted in place, paralysed by fear.

The bear nudged him gently, a surprising contrast to its fearsome appearance. Slowly, it manoeuvred him out of the cockpit, guiding him away from the twisted metal. Finnian stumbled, still disoriented, but the bear's insistence was clear.

Once Finnian was out of the plane, the bear paused, its colossal form blocking the wreckage from him. For a moment, it simply stood there, as if ensuring the man was safe. Then, with a final, almost reluctant glance, the bear turned and walked back into the forest.

Finnian watched in stunned silence, his mind struggling to process what had just happened. The bear's silhouette merged with the shadows of the trees, but before it disappeared entirely, it turned back to look at him one last time.

The weight of the encounter pressed heavily on Finnian's mind. Had he been saved by a force he had feared? Was the bear a guardian in the guise of a predator? Why hadn't it eaten him when it had the opportunity? As he stood alone in the clearing of trees, metres from the wreckage of the plane, he couldn't help but feel perplexed by the unexpected mercy of the bear.

A vast expanse of green forest loomed before Finnian, appearing to consume the entire horizon. He stumbled forward, his legs unsteady from the crash, the pungent scent of gas still clinging to his nostrils. Each step was an effort, not just from his physical injuries, but from the weight of memories that pressed down upon him like an invisible burden.

Moving further into the wilderness, the trees enveloped him, their branches extending like twisted fingers. The light dimmed as it filtered through the leafy canopy, casting dappled shadows on the ground of the forest. Finnian's mind wandered, slipping between the present moment and the haunting echoes of his splintered past.

The bitter tang of fear rose in his throat as he remembered the bear. The prickling realization cast him back to his reality. He took a deep breath, trying to steady himself as he surveyed the surroundings.

The forest was an impenetrable fortress, the towering trees casting shadows that seemed to stretch for miles. The symphony of wildlife that surrounded him was now a cacophony of danger, each bird call and rustling leaf a warning of the dangers lurking within.

As he spun around in a panicked frenzy, his mind raced with thoughts of survival. The beauty and serenity he had seen from above were now replaced with a sense of overwhelming dread and isolation. The desolate landscape offered no succour, no reprieve from the overwhelming feeling of fear that consumed him. Emerging from prison only three days ago, he had never felt so alone. Now, he stumbled through a barren wasteland, a new kind of prison that seemed to suffocate him with its emptiness and deafening silence that threatened to drive him mad. His isolation was a constant reminder of his past mistakes and the daunting uncertainty of his future.

He gazed back toward the wreckage of the plane, realizing it held only temporary shelter. The forest held both his salvation and his demise, a reminder of his fragile mortality. Every step he took could mean life or death.

A deep sense of desperation consumed him. He felt a physical ache in his chest, as if the weight of the forest were crushing down on him. This was not merely a physical challenge; it was an emotional torment. Each tree and shadow taunted him. Tears pricked his eyes, a mixture of anger and sorrow for losing control and the uncertainty that loomed ahead.

Every muscle in Finnian's body screamed with pain as he stumbled through the dense forest, his heart pounding in his chest. His eyes scanned the towering trees, searching for any sign of escape. Suddenly, a glimmer caught his eye - a tall tree with thick branches that seemed strong enough to hold his weight. With a fierce drive burning deep inside him, Finnian pushed himself towards the tree. The crash had left him battered and bruised, but his will to survive was unbreakable. Clutching the coarse bark of the lowest limb, he hoisted himself up with a grunt of effort.

The ascent was treacherous; each bought a new challenge to overcome. The rough bark, blood mixing with sweat as he pulled himself higher and higher, tore into his hands. With every step he took, the view in front of him grew wider.

Finally reaching a vantage point where he could see over the treetops, Finnian's heart sank. An endless sea of green stretched out in every direction, with no sign of civilization or rescue, nothing he might not have seen while flying overhead. He felt defeated as he grasped the true extent of his solitude and abandonment.

Clinging to the branch above, Finnian felt the weight of it all pressing down on him - the physical exhaustion and emotional despair. But something ignited within him - a fierce tenacity to survive against all odds.

He began his descent from the tree. As he stood on solid ground once again,

Finnian looked back at the towering canopy above. He had felt so truly lonely.

Finnian's body ached with every movement, his muscles sore from the impact of the crash. Yet, he knew he had to press on. Survival depended on it, and the sun was already disappearing. He scanned the forest floor. The rustling leaves and distant calls of wildlife guided his steps as he traversed through the dense greenery. His determined search for a reliable shelter led him to follow the gentle sound of a stream. Running water. He hurried to the stream and thrust his hands into the icy water. Despite its frigid temperature, he couldn't resist taking a few gulps to satisfy his thirst.

The water glistened in the fading light, the forest beckoning Finnian further. And there, nestled in the side of the mountain, was an earthen cave, its walls formed by compacted dirt and intertwined roots. Without hesitation, Finnian claimed the dugout, moving quickly.

As twilight descended upon the forest, Finnian set to work fortifying his shelter. Sturdy branches were gathered and strategically placed at the mouth of the cave, providing additional support and protection from the elements. Over this framework, he layered leafy branches, creating a natural camouflage that would also provide warmth.

With careful attention to detail, he added a layer of plump moss over the exterior of his shelter, ensuring maximum insulation against cold winds. Inside, he carefully crafted a bed made of soft leaves.

The shelter was crude but would provide some protection. He settled into the trench, the branches overhead creating a rough barrier against the sky. The forest around him was alive with the sounds of night; birdcall, insects buzzing and chirping, leaves rustling, the distant call of an owl.

He continued moving, collecting dry leaves, twigs, and small branches in a careful pile. His fingers trembled as he rubbed two sticks together, trying to generate enough heat to light the kindling. Each failed attempt only added to his frustration. The strain in his muscles seemed to seep into his bones, draining his strength. Despite his efforts, the twigs remained stubbornly unlit due to the moisture in the air and dampness of the forest floor working against him. Finnian's breath came in ragged gasps; exhaustion and despair weighing heavily on him. As darkness surrounded him and the cold seeped through his thin clothes, he knew he needed fire for warmth, light, and protection. But it remained out of reach. He tried different combinations of materials and adjusted the pile, but still no luck.

Finnian refused to give up despite his aching muscles as he kept drilling the twigs. His hands grew blistered, but finally, a spark caught. Holding his breath, he gently coaxed it and fed it with tiny splinters of wood until a small flame emerged. With relief coursing through him, Finnian sat back as the fire grew and crackled larger. The warm glow cast shadows around him, offering relief in the vast darkness of the forest.

Exhausted but determined, he leaned against the dirt wall of his shelter with the fire's warmth penetrating his body. The day's ordeal had taken its toll, but for now, he had shelter and a fire to keep him going through the night. As he watched the flames dance before him, Finnian felt a spark ignite within himself. He would survive one difficult step at a time. Eventually, sleep overtook him as darkness fully enveloped the forest and he settled by the fire's comforting warmth.

GRACE

Grace sat at the kitchen table, her hands gripping a mug of scalding hot tea in an effort to calm her racing thoughts. It had been a week since she had last heard from Finnian, and each passing minute felt like an eternity. Worry gnawed at her insides like a ravenous beast, threatening to consume her. The house felt too quiet, too empty without her son's presence.

Suddenly, Patrick strode into the room, his expression as stoic and unreadable as ever. Grace's heart clenched with desperation as she turned to him. "Patrick, it's been a week. I haven't heard a word from Finnian. I'm scared," she choked out.

But Patrick's response was cold and dismissive. "He's probably just out with friends. Remember, he's still on parole after spending two years in prison." Tears sprang to Grace's eyes as she shook her head vehemently. "No, something doesn't seem right." What if he's in trouble? We have to do something."

Patrick's jaw tightened, annoyance crossing his face. "You need to stop hovering over him. He's an adult now."

Grace's frustration boiled over, leading her to be unable to hold back any longer. "I know he's an adult, but he's still our son! How can you be so apathetic?" But Patrick remained silent, his gaze fixed on some distant point as if he wasn't even present in the room. The weight of their unspoken disagreement hung heavy in the air between them, a suffocating presence that threatened to break them apart.

Despite Patrick's words, Grace struggled to rid herself of the sense that something terrible had happened to Finnian. She knew she had to keep searching for answers, for any indication of where he might be and how to bring him back home. Her tenacity burned bright even as her heart was consumed by fear and worry.

Without another word, she grasped her keys and headed out the door.

FINNIAN

Finnian jolted awake, a sharp pang of hunger gnawing at his stomach. He sat up and took in his surroundings with bleary eyes. The forest was alive with the sounds of morning - birds chirping in the trees above and rabbits scurrying through the underbrush.

The growling of his stomach reminded Finnian that he needed to find something to eat. His gaze fell upon a cluster of thin but sturdy sticks on the ground. After propelling himself upright, he gingerly plucked the sticks from the tree.

Back at his shelter, he had a piece of metal from the plane wreck waiting for him. With a rock, he honed it into a makeshift blade. He shaped the ends of the sticks, the rhythmic sound of metal scraping against wood filling the air. Each spear took form under his skilled touch, sharpened to effective points. Driven by hunger, Finnian worked swiftly and soon had a bundle of spears ready for hunting.

A feeling of contentment mixed with his enduring appetite. Finnian tested the weight and balance of one spear in his hand before looking out at the sun dappled forest. Today, he would find sustenance. Today, he would survive.

With his bundle of spears in tow, Finnian stepped into the forest with perseverance. The journey of survival was far from over, but with each step, he grew more attuned to the rhythms of nature and stronger in his abilities. The forest was both foe and friend - a place full of danger but also potential nourishment - and Finnian was determined to overcome its challenges.

An hour had slipped by unnoticed, and Finnian's empty stomach grumbled audibly, a reminder of his urgent need for sustenance. He moved quietly through the dense undergrowth of the forest, scanning for any sign of prey to quell his hunger. Despite his sharpened spears and skilled aim, every attempt at catching something had been in vain.

As he trudged on, the rays of the morning sun filtered through the trees, casting patterns of light and shadow on the forest floor. The birds continued their carefree melodies, unaware of his unfruitful efforts.

Just when he was about to give up hope, Finnian's sharp eyes caught sight of a small rabbit nibbling on some grass. With bated breath, he crouched low and aimed at one of his spears.

With a calculated throw, the spear sailed through the air and struck its target with precision. The rabbit fell lifelessly to the ground, and Finnian felt a rush of relief and gratitude. He approached cautiously and confirmed that the animal was indeed dead before retrieving it.

The weight of the rabbit in his hands brought a sense of accomplishment, a hard-earned prize for his ambition. In silent appreciation for the forest's provision, he whispered thanks as he prepared to take what he needed to survive. With newfound energy and purpose, Finnian returned to his shelter with his catch in hand. Rekindling his fire, he set about cleaning and cooking the rabbit over the flames. The scent of roasting meat filled the air.

Sitting by the fire, Finnian savoured each bite of his meal, grateful for the resources that had sustained him.
Finnian's initial triumph of catching and cooking a rabbit quickly turned to despair. As he finished his meal, a sudden wave of nausea hit him with full force. He clutched at his stomach, the cramps intensifying with each passing moment.

The realization that the rabbit must have been carrying a parasite only added to his misery.

The next twelve hours were a blur of agony. Finnian lay on the ground, curled into a tight ball as he tried to fight off the relentless waves of nausea. Each time he thought it was over; another bout would hit him with even more ferocity. He could feel every muscle in his body tense up before he was overcome by violent retching and vomiting. His skin was slick with sweat and his entire body shook with each convulsion.

Despite his weakened state, Finnian managed to tend to his fire and take shelter in his makeshift camp. But even there, he couldn't escape the grip of sickness as he drifted in and out of consciousness, unable to find any relief from his suffering.

THE BEAR

The bear watched silently from the distant trees as the man doubled over in pain and sickness. The sight triggered something in the bear. Without hesitation, the great animal turned and dashed into the depths of the forest with its powerful legs carrying it effortlessly through the undergrowth.

For an hour, the bear scoured the forest floor in search for something that could help the man. It used its keen sense of smell to guide it to a patch of ripe wild blackberries. The bear plucked a mouthful of berries from the bush, gently carrying them in its mouth until it could hold no more. With a sense of urgency, it returned to the man's camp.

Approaching cautiously, the bear noticed the comforting warmth of the campfire against the chilly night air. It gingerly placed the wild blackberries near the fire, hoping that the man would find them and be nourished. However, as it glanced towards the shelter, it saw that the man was sound asleep inside, breathing peacefully. The bear retreated back into the safety of the forest.

BAREE

Baree sat on her couch, mindlessly swiping through her phone as the day's buzz died down and the evening settled in. Suddenly, her heart skipped a beat when Finnian's name in her notifications caught her eye. She eagerly tapped on the message, a smile spreading across her face as she read his words.

"Out of town, back tonight. Want to catch up?"

Her chest warmed with excitement and a fluttering sensation filled her stomach - emotions she hadn't experienced in a long time. With quick typing fingers, Baree sent him a simple but heartfelt reply: a smiley face.

She couldn't suppress the feelings of anticipation and happiness bubbling inside her as she leaned back against the cushions. She was eager to see Finnian once more, to carry on their easy conversations. For the first time in a while, Baree realized she was missing this kind of connection.

Filled with contentment and gratitude for new beginnings, she gently placed her phone down with a smile lingering on her lips, allowing herself to soak in the warmth of potential love and meaningful connections.

FINNIAN

Finnian woke from his sickness-induced slumber, his body aching and his mouth dry. As he blinked his eyes open, a faint, sweet aroma that seemed out of place in the forest greeted him. The smell of cooking sugar tickled his senses, stirring him from his daze.

He sat up slowly, his muscles protesting with every movement. The fire nearby had burned low, but it still emitted enough heat to keep him warm. As he shifted, Finnian noticed something strange near the fire, a small pile of blackberries glistening in the dim light.

Curiosity piqued, he crawled closer, the sweet scent growing stronger. The berries sizzled and caramelised as they were placed so close to the fire, creating the intoxicating smell that piqued his curiosity and roused him.

With a shaky hand, he picked up a few berries and popped them into his mouth. The burst of sweet and tart flavours was a welcome relief, soothing his parched throat and invigorating his senses. He ate slowly, savouring each berry as it melted on his tongue.

As he ate, Finnian couldn't help but wonder how the berries had gotten there. He glanced around the clearing, his gaze falling on the tree line where the bear often watched him. A thought crossed his mind, could the bear have brought the berries for him?

The idea seemed almost too fantastical, yet the evidence was there.

Finnian leaned back against the dirt wall of his shelter. With a deep breath, he closed his eyes, feeling the fatigue of the past hours slowly ebb away. As he nodded off to sleep, he could no longer escape the feeling that the bear was indeed watching him.

Finnian awoke to the relentless grip of hunger, gnawing at his insides like a starving beast. The meagre handful of blackberries he had eaten the night before only served as a cruel reminder of his desperate situation. But he refused to give in, determined to find more.

The morning sun filtered through the dense canopy, casting an eerie light over the forest floor. Finnian moved with caution and purpose; his senses heightened as he searched for any signs of edible plants.

The forest was alive with the chirping of birds and rustling of animals, but Finnian's focus remained unshaken. He followed his instincts, tracking the faint scent of fresh berries deeper into the thick undergrowth. His body weak from sickness and injury, he pushed himself forward without hesitation.

Finally, after what seemed like an endless journey, Finnian caught sight of a cluster of berry bushes in the distance. With renewed energy, he sprinted towards them, his heart pounding in anticipation. As he drew closer, he could see that the bushes were full to bursting with juicy, ripe fruit.

His instincts told him to be cautious, but hunger overruled caution. He reached out, picking a handful of berries, their vibrant hues promising a sweet relief. He quickly began filling his shirt with as many berries as he could gather. Finnian's mind wandered back to a simpler time, a day etched in his memory with the warmth and sweetness of blackberry pies. He and John were eight or nine, the world full of endless possibilities and adventures. They had spent the afternoon in Igrit's cozy kitchen, the aroma of baking pies filling the air.

Igrit's hands moved deftly as she rolled out the dough, her laughter echoing in the room. The boys, with makeshift swords crafted from broomsticks and cardboard, were deep in their own imaginary battle. The clanging of their 'weapons and their playful shouts created a symphony of childhood joy.

"En Garde!" John exclaimed, lunging towards Finnian, who parried the attack with a grin. They darted around the kitchen, careful not to bump into Igrit as she worked her culinary magic. Occasionally, she would glance over at them, a loving smile on her face.

When the pies were finally ready, Igrit pulled them from the oven, their golden crusts glistening, with bubbling, dark purple filling peeking through. She cut generous slices for the boys, who immediately abandoned their swords and gathered at the table. The first bite was a burst of flavour, sweet, tart, and comforting all at once.

As they devoured their pie, the boys exchanged stories of heroic deeds and grand quests. Igrit listened, her heart full, as she cleaned up the kitchen. The sun dipped lower in the sky, casting a warm glow through the window, wrapping them all in its embrace. Finnian held onto that memory, a beacon of happiness in the tumultuous times that followed.

His recollection was cut short by a familiar sound. Just as he reached out to pluck a berry from its branch, a low growl sounded behind him. He froze, slowly turning to come face to face with a hulking bear, its eyes trained on him with deadly intent. Despite his fear and exhaustion, Finnian stood his ground, not knowing how to react to the shadow that loomed before him.

BAREE

As Baree waited for Finnian's reply, she cast her mind back to the night on the jetty. The marina was quiet, the occasional sound of lapping water the only noise interrupting the stillness. As they walked along the pier, Finnian felt a comfortable silence settle between them. Then, Baree took a deep breath, as if gathering the courage to speak.

"Finnian, there's something I need to tell you," She began, her voice soft but resolute. "I grew up in a small coastal town. My dad was a fisherman, and my mum ran a bookstore. I spent so many hours in that shop, lost in books, dreaming of adventures far away."

Finnian listened intently; his eyes fixed on her as she continued. "When my dad passed away, I stayed close to help my mom. But I always had this itch to explore. Eventually, I saved enough to travel. I hiked through forests, camped under starlit skies, and swam in the ocean. I found so much peace in nature. It's where I feel most at home."

She paused, looking out at the boats bobbing gently in the marina. "But there's more. I got married young. Thought I knew him, I was wrong. He turned out to be abusive. I managed to leave after six months. It wasn't easy, but it made me stronger. I vowed never to let anyone dim my spirit again." Finnian reached out, gently squeezing her hand.

She smiled, the moonlight catching the glint in her eyes. "I want you to know, Finnian. We all have our pasts. They shape us, but they don't define us."

They sat down at the end of the pier, the weight of their shared stories mingling with the tranquillity of the night. In the distance, the faint hum of the club was a reminder of a world they had temporarily stepped away from, finding solace in each other's company.

THE BEAR

The bear wandered through its familiar territory; its keen eyes ever watchful. The scents and sounds of the forest were a comforting symphony, a guide to its daily life. As it moved, the bear's attention was drawn to the man, who had stumbled upon a bush of bright berries.

The bear's memory flashed back to a time when it had once consumed those same berries, their vibrant colours deceiving it into thinking they were a safe meal. The aftermath had been excruciating. Days of sickness followed a deep pain in its stomach and a haze clouding its mind. The lesson was seared into its instincts; those berries were dangerous.

From its vantage point, the bear watched as the man began picking the berries, filling his shirt with the tempting, yet toxic, fruit. The bear grunted, a low warning that rumbled through the still forest air. The human, oblivious to the danger, grunted back, "I'm hungry."

Distress surged through the bear. It rose up on its hind legs, growling louder, its massive form a shadow of urgency. It pawed at the ground, trying to communicate the peril to the man. But the man continued, driven by hunger, unaware of the threat.

Seeing no other choice, the bear charged furiously towards him. The sudden movement and the bear's powerful presence startled him, causing the berries to spill from his shirt as he fled in a panic. The bear's growls echoed through the trees; its frustration physical.

Once the man was at a safe distance, the bear approached the scattered berries. It needed to ensure they would not be consumed. With a deliberate motion, the bear defecated on the berries, marking them as inedible. Then, in a final act of instinctual finality, the bear flicked dirt over the mess with its back feet, much like a dog marking its territory. The man stood watching, his mind a tumult of bewilderment and a disgust.

"Right then," the man spoke, his hands now on his hips,

"I suppose the berries you left me last night were okay?" he queried in rhetoric.

The bear turned and walked a few steps away, beckoning the man to follow. Fuelled by curiosity and the blackberries in mind, he trailed after the bear into the depths of the forest.

The bear moved with purpose, gliding effortlessly through the dense underbrush. The man struggled to keep up, but his ambition outweighed any physical discomfort. They ventured deeper into the forest, the tall trees above casting intricate patterns of light and shadow on the ground below. The air was thick with earthy scents. The bear led him down meandering paths, each turn revealing more dense trees and shrubbery.

They soon arrived at a small clearing surrounded by towering trees. The man approached cautiously, not knowing what to expect. But as soon as he caught sight of it, his eyes lit up with delight. In front of him lay a vast expanse of blackberry bushes, heavy with ripe fruit that glistened in the sunlight. The bear sat back, observing with quiet satisfaction as the man eagerly gathered berries from the bushes and filled his shirt with them. The sweet and tangy aroma filled the air. He then proceeded to place a handful of them in his mouth, each ball of goodness popping beneath the pressure of his teeth.

The man, filled with gratitude, softly whispered his thanks to the bear.

FINNIAN

Finnian cautiously navigated through the twisted metal and shattered glass, his boots crunching loudly with each step. The acrid stench of gas filled his nostrils, causing him to gag as he pushed forward into the wreckage. He rummaged through debris, hoping to find anything salvageable. Inside the aircraft, he found his backpack that he had stashed behind a seat before taking off.

His fingers brushed against an old cassette tape and without hesitation, he put on the headphones, and pressed play. To his surprise, the cassette started playing. Drowning out the chaos around him with the familiar static, he became lost in his search. He failed to notice the towering presence of the bear watching from a distance with dark, curious eyes.

He filled his pack with usable items - a partially full canteen, a first aid kit, and a small knife-like tin can opener.

As Finnian scoured further into the plane, he stumbled upon an old, weathered book wedged between the seats. The cover, once vibrant, was now faded and tattered. He brushed off the dirt and squinted at the title, feeling a spark of recognition. It was 'The Fellowship of the Ring' by J.R.R. Tolkien.

A faint smile crossed his lips as he flipped through the pages, the familiar words stirring memories of distant lands and epic journeys. He tucked the book into his pack, satisfied with his haul.

As he turned to leave, his heart stopped at the sight of the large bear just a few meters away. Its furry silhouette blended into the surrounding forest, making it difficult for Finnian to distinguish between friend or foe in this unpredictable and dangerous situation.

Without warning, Finnian was suddenly attacked by a wolf from the shadows. The beast snapped at his legs, sending him crashing to the ground with a thud.

But before he could even take a breath, the bear charged in with unrestrained force. It was a chaotic blur of teeth and fur as they battled fiercely for dominance. Finnian watched helplessly as the two predators clashed until finally, the bear emerged victorious with a deafening roar that shook him to his core.

Feeling vulnerable and exposed, Finnian scrambled for cover as he made a desperate sprint towards the nearest tree. With adrenaline coursing through his veins, he climbed frantically while watching with awe and fear as the bear reclaimed its territory in the clearing once again.

As their gazes met, Finnian couldn't help but feel a surge of emotions - fear, awe, and ultimately, respect for the untamed and wild creature before him. As the winds lashed against his face and branches creaked under his weight, Finnian pondered this question in the midst of survival at its most raw and intense form - was it really just a protector or something more sinister?

THE BEAR

The bear watched the man's movements with curious eyes as he searched through the debris of the crashed plane. It sat silently at the edge of the forest, hidden from view as it observed his every move. The scent of fear and ambition emanated from the man, filling the bear's sensitive nose.

Minutes passed in eerie silence before a loud howl shattered the peace. The bear recognised it as a warning - wolves were nearby. Without hesitation, it stepped out into the open, letting out a fierce bark to warn both the man and any potential attackers. But it was too late. A pack of six wolves had already surrounded the clearing.

With ferocity and strength beyond measure, the bear fought off two wolves that dared to attack first. Its massive jaws clamped down on one wolf's neck, shaking it until it lay lifeless on the ground. The second wolf met a swift swipe from its powerful paw, sending it flying into a nearby tree. Injured but determined, the wolf tried once more to attack, only to be pinned down by the bear's weight and finished with a final bite.

But there was no time for rest, as more danger lurked nearby. The bear spotted the largest wolf creeping up behind the man near the wreckage of the plane. With lightning speed, it lunged forward and knocked the wolf off course just as it prepared to attack from behind. The man continued his task, oblivious to the intense battle that had taken place behind him under the watchful protection of a courageous but unseen ally.

Aggressive and determined, the bear attacked the wolf with all its might, sinking its enormous teeth into the smaller animal's throat and ravaging its vulnerable flesh. The wolf put up a valiant fight, snapping back at its attacker as blood gushed from its wounds. Yet, the bear relentlessly attacked, a primal force that could not be defeated. With one final, powerful shake, the wolf went limp in the bear's grasp. As steam rose from its hot breath, the predator let out a victorious roar and breathed heavily in the cold air. Its fierce eyes dared any other challenger to come forward.

The remaining wolves backed away, witnessing the brutal display of dominance. Two injured wolves whimpered and retreated; their bodies covered in deep gashes. The others cautiously circled around, sensing that this was a battle they could not win.

But one young male wolf, driven by bravery or foolishness, charged at the bear with a snarl. The bear met him head-on, swiping with massive paws that left bloody trails across his face and body. Yelping in pain, the young wolf eventually fled with his tail between his legs.

Satisfied that it had defended its territory and vanquished its enemies, the bear turned its attention back to the man. Oblivious to the intense struggle that had just taken place behind him, he remained peacefully asleep near his plane. Dragging the lifeless body of the largest wolf into the shadows of the forest, the powerful predator discarded it with ease. Returning to its post just a few meters away from the man and his plane, the great guardian sat down with a silent growl rumbling deep within its chest. It kept watch over its domain and those within it as darkness descended upon the forest.

BAREE

Finnian's mother clutched her coat tightly as she stepped into the dimly lit bar. The weight of worry had settled heavily on her shoulders over the past three months. Finnian had vanished without a trace, and the only lead they had was his last transaction, at this very bar. Her heart pounded as she scanned the room, searching for any sign of promise.

The bar was a mix of shadows and soft light, patrons murmuring in low voices. She spotted the bartender, a young woman with a warm but weary expression, tending to a customer. Taking a deep breath, she approached the bar.

"Excuse me," she said, her voice trembling slightly. "Are you Baree?"

The woman looked up, her eyes widening with recognition. "Yes, that's me. How can I help you?"

Finnian's mother hesitated, her emotions threatening to overwhelm her. "I'm Finnian's mother. The police told me his last transaction was here, three months ago. He's been missing since then. I was hoping you might remember something, anything, that could help us find him."

Baree's heart was torn in two as she was hit with a wave of shock. A sense of tension consumed her.

"Of course," she replied, blinking rapidly, "Wait...he's missing?"

Tears welled up in Finnian's mother's eyes. "Did he say where he was going? Did he mention anything at all?"

Baree shook her head slowly. "No, he didn't. I'm so sorry. I've been worried about him too. He hasn't responded to any of my messages."

As they spoke, Baree's ex-partner, seated at the bar, overheard the conversation. His brow furrowed in concern, and he quietly listened in, trying to piece together any details that might help. Finnian's mother glanced around the bar, feeling the emptiness of the lead slipping through her fingers. "Thank you," she whispered, her voice barely audible. "Thank you for trying to help."

Baree reached out, placing a comforting hand on her arm. "I wish I could do more. If anything comes to mind, anything at all, I'll let you know. We'll find him, I promise."

Finnian's mother nodded, her heart aching with a mixture of faith and despair. She turned to leave, the sense of loss deepening with every step. The bar door closed behind her, but the search for her son was far from over. She would keep looking, keep hoping, until she brought him home.

Baree's colleague approached her, his expression a mix of curiosity and concern.

"What was that about?" he asked cautiously.

Baree shook her head, struggling to make sense of it all. "That was Finnian's mother."

"Finnian?"

"Yeah, I told you about him."

"Oh, the guy that came in here looking for you."

"She was asking about him using his debit card here three months ago. It's been three months since anyone has heard from him."

Her colleague's eyes widened. "Three months? That's a long time to be off the grid. Do you think he's okay?"

Baree's heart clenched with fear. "I don't know. I've got to go."

As the worry consumed her, Baree grabbed her phone and checked her messages. Her heart sank when she saw that none of her messages to Finnian had been delivered. The little grey checkmarks next to each one were a stark reminder of the growing distance between them and the uncertainty surrounding Finnian's disappearance.

She had convinced herself that he had simply ghosted her after their last meeting and stopped reaching out a month ago. But now, faced with the reality of his absence, she couldn't ignore the sinking feeling in her gut. What had happened to Finnian? Why hadn't he responded? The silence felt suffocating, and Baree couldn't shake off the fear that something terrible had happened to him. Baree's colleague placed a reassuring hand on her shoulder. "I'm sure he's okay. Maybe he just needs some time alone. Let's not jump to conclusions."

Baree nodded, but deep down she knew she couldn't just let this go.

Baree could feel the tension simmering as soon as she walked through the front door. Just then, she heard the unmistakable sound of the door creaking open behind her. She turned to see her ex-husband standing there, a storm brewing in his eyes, having just overheard her conversation at the bar.

"Who is Finnian?" he blurted out, his voice tight with suspicion. "Is he someone you're seeing behind my back?"

Baree sighed, exhaustion weighing her down. She didn't want to have this conversation, not now, not ever. "He's a customer, nothing more," she lied, her tone measured. "He came into the bar, and that's the last I saw of him."

"Are you sure about that?" He crossed his arms, his gaze piercing. "Because it seems like you know a lot about him. Enough to help his mother, at least."

She met his gaze, her expression hardening. "We're divorced, remember? We just share this house until we figure things out. My life isn't your concern anymore."

His eyes flashed with anger. "It's still my business if you're bringing other men into our lives."

Baree shook her head, frustration bubbling up. "I'm not bringing anyone into our lives. Finnian was a customer, that's it. His mother came in looking for him, and I did what any decent person would do; tried to help. Stop making this about you."

He looked away, the tension in the room thick enough to cut. Baree felt a pang of regret, but also a steely resolve. Her life was her own, and she wouldn't let his insecurities control her anymore.

"Look," she said, her voice softening, "We both need space to figure things out. Let's not make this harder than it has to be."

Without a word, she spun on her heel and began to march away, leaving him to stew in his own dark thoughts. But suddenly, he sprang into action, closing the distance between them in a matter of seconds. With one violent lunge, he grabbed a fistful of her hair, jerking her head back with a sickening crunch. His other hand clamped onto her face, crushing her face against the rough stone wall behind her. A guttural moan escaped her lips as blood gushed from her broken nose and split forehead, staining the ground red as she crumpled to the floor in a heap.

FINNIAN

The days in the forest often blended together, each one marked by a rhythm of routine and subtle changes. With each new day, Finnian found solace in the mundane tasks that kept him grounded. The sunrise would find him trekking through the forest, gathering firewood with a purposeful stride. The repetitive act of collecting sticks and branches had become a meditative ritual, allowing him to clear his mind and focus on the present.

As he cooked his modest breakfast of foraged berries and whatever game he had caught, he would feel the warm sun on his back and listen to the peaceful sounds of the forest. The soft crunch of leaves underfoot, the gentle rustle of small animals scurrying about, all added to the tranquil atmosphere. After his meal, Finnian would spend hours reinforcing his shelter. The simple structure required constant maintenance, but it gave him something to do with his hands and something to concentrate on. He took pride in his work, creating a sturdy home in the heart of nature.

A steady rhythm of activity and stillness marked the passing hours. There were no sudden bursts of excitement or dramatic events in this quiet corner of the world. Instead, time seemed to move at a gentler pace, guided by the predictable rising and setting of the sun.

In the afternoons, when time allowed, Finnian would retreat to a peaceful spot by a lake or beneath the shade of a tall tree. He would pull out John's old, weathered copy of *The Fellowship of the Ring* and lose himself in its familiar words. With each turn of the page, he transported himself to another world filled with adventure and wonder. It was a welcome escape from his own solitary existence.

The book had become his anchor, a constant companion in the solitude of the forest. He would read for hours on end, savouring every sentence as he immersed himself in the epic journey of Frodo and Gandalf. And sometimes, as he reflected on their quests, he couldn't help but draw parallels to his own search for redemption and peace.

As the sun set, Finnian would settle in front of his crackling fire with a sense of calm. The dancing flames cast a mesmerizing glow over his surroundings, making everything feel more alive. In those quiet moments, he would let his thoughts drift aimlessly, finding comfort in the simplicity and beauty of the forest.

The sun hung low in the sky, casting a warm golden hue over the tranquil lake. The water sparkled like diamonds, reflecting the vibrant colours of the sunset. Finnian stood at the edge of the lake, the cool water lapping gently against his bare feet. He gazed out at the peaceful expanse, taking in the natural beauty around him.

As he waded into the shallow edge, Finnian felt a sense of calm wash over him. He closed his eyes and let the soothing sound of the water, and the gentle breeze fill his senses. As if drawn by some invisible force, he cupped his hands and splashed water over his face, feeling refreshed and renewed.

But then he heard it, a soft rustling in the nearby underbrush. He opened his eyes and turned towards the sound, heart pounding with trepidation. Emerging from the trees was a sight that took his breath away, a mother bear followed closely by her cub.

They moved with a graceful ease, their powerful bodies gliding through the undergrowth like dancers on a stage.

Finnian watched in awe as they made their way along the lakeshore, their majestic presence reflecting the untamed beauty of nature.

Despite the danger that lurked beneath their wild exterior, there was an undeniable tenderness between mother and cub. The little bear trotted playfully beside its mother, occasionally stumbling but always quickly regaining its balance. Finnian couldn't help but smile at the endearing display.

He remained still, not wanting to disturb their peaceful journey. The mother bear glanced in his direction, her deep brown eyes seeming to look right into his soul. For a moment, time seemed to stand still as they shared this quiet moment together.

As they continued their path along the shore, Finnian's heart swelled with a mix of reverence and gratitude. This encounter was a reminder of the simple yet profound beauty of nature, the kind that exists beyond the chaos and complexities of human life. Still, a feeling of sadness erupted within him as he remembered the mother and child who died in the car crash.

Two years had passed since the accident, but for Finnian, the memories were still raw and unyielding. A shiver ran through him as he approached the lake where the two lives had been lost. The trees seemed to whisper accusations as he stepped out of his car, carrying a bouquet of white lilies and a teddy bear. He couldn't help but wonder if those who had gathered at a distance were judging him, their murmurs feeling like sharp arrows aimed at his already fractured heart. Kneeling down beside the marker, Finnian placed the flowers and teddy bear at its base. He tried to focus on offering his apologies and seeking forgiveness, but thoughts of what others must think of him consumed his mind. Did they see him as a monster? A killer? Would they ever be able to forgive him for the tragedy he caused?

The silence of the forest seemed to amplify his doubts and fears. His tears fell as he whispered his plea for redemption. "I'm sorry," he choked out, his voice breaking under the weight of his emotions. "I hope you can find peace wherever you are."

But even as he spoke those words, Finnian couldn't help but doubt if he would ever find peace himself. Would anyone ever be able to look past his mistakes and see the man he was today?

As he stood up and walked back to his car, Finnian couldn't shake off the feeling of being watched by judgmental eyes. The glances and whispers of those who saw him only as a criminal added to the heaviness in his chest.

As he looked up from the lake, broken from his thoughts, he was grateful in that moment to be alone, to be free of judgement and ridicule.

The mother bear and her cub disappeared into the trees, leaving him alone again. The lake's waters gently embraced him, and Finnian closed his eyes, letting the moment seep into his soul. It was in these fleeting, precious encounters with the wild that he found solace.

Finnian knelt by the river, the cold-water swirling around his hands as he scrubbed his clothes against a smooth rock. The rhythmic motion and the sound of the flowing water were almost meditative, providing a brief respite from the challenges of survival. All of a sudden, he observed a shift in the water's current. It seemed to grow stronger, more insistent. Finnian paused, glancing upstream. The river, which had been relatively calm moments ago, was now teeming with movement.

The sound hit him next, a deep, roaring rumble that filled the air. Finnian's heart quickened as he realised what was happening. The salmon run had begun, and the river was alive with the thrashing bodies of countless fish, all surging upstream in their ancient migration. The sky awoke in a frenzy of flapping wings and eager beaks as birds came from every direction, diving and swooping, plucking fish from the water.

He gazed in awe as the salmon leaped and darted through the water, their silvery bodies flashing in the sunlight. The sheer number of them was staggering. The river seemed to boil with life, the sound of their struggle against the current vibrating through the forest.

Finnian stood; his wet clothes forgotten, captivated by the spectacle. He had read about the salmon run but seeing it in person was a unique experience entirely. The power and urgency of the salmon's journey filled him with a sense of wonder and respect for the natural world.

The river, now a churning torrent of fish, transformed into a bustling artery of life. The salmon's desperate leaps and frantic dashes created a mesmerizing display of raw energy and tenacity. Finnian sensed the vibrations through the ground, the sheer force of the run pulsing through his feet. The noise was deafening, a symphony of splashing water and frenzied movement that echoed through the trees. As he kept watching, a sudden thought popped into his mind. This abundance of salmon could be a crucial source of food for him as winter approached. The challenge would be finding a way to catch them, but the opportunity was too significant to ignore.

Finnian's mind raced, adrenaline surging through his veins. He waded into the water, the icy current tugging at him as he positioned himself strategically. With a makeshift spear in hand, he watched the salmon, their sleek bodies flashing by in a blur of motion. Summoning every ounce of focus and resolution, he struck. His spear met its mark, piercing the side of a large salmon. The fish thrashed wildly, its strength surprising him, but he held on, sensing a rush of triumph course through him.

He pulled the salmon from the water, its scales glistening in the sunlight. The exhilaration of the hunt and the thrill of success were intoxicating. The river had provided a gift, and he intended to make the most of it. The salmon run was a reminder that even in the wild, nature had a way of offering sustenance to those who were willing to see it.

A subtle shift in the atmosphere alerted his senses. A low growl, almost imperceptible but unmistakable, rumbled through the air. He turned, his eyes scanning the forest floor, and there, through a break in the trees, he saw it; a black bear, majestic and formidable, ambling through the underbrush. As he secured his catch, Finnian glanced upstream and saw the grey bear.

It moved with grace and precision, swiping its paw into the water and emerging with a large salmon clasped in its jaws. It retreated to a flat, slate-covered section of the riverbank, settling down to enjoy its meal.

Finnian watched, intrigued, as the bear began to eat. To his surprise, the bear only consumed the brain and the skin of the salmon, leaving the rest of the fish untouched. The bear's careful selection fascinated him, and he wondered why it ignored the rest of the nutritious flesh.

Seeing an opportunity, Finnian approached cautiously, his eyes on the bear. The bear seemed focused on its next meal, but as Finnian moved closer, it lifted its head, eyes narrowing.

Finnian hesitated, then took another step forward, intending to salvage the remains of the bear's discarded meal.

The bear growled low in its throat, a sound that resonated through the air. Finnian stopped in his tracks, sensing the bear's warning. Despite his curiosity and hunger, he knew better than to challenge the bear. Reluctantly, he backed away, watching as the bear finished its chosen parts of the fish before wandering off into the forest.

Puzzled by the bear's behaviour, Finnian returned to his own catch, the mystery lingering in his mind. He discarded his catch and turned in the direction of the blackberry grove.

THE BEAR

The bear stood like a looming shadow, its massive form blending into the darkness. The scent of the wolves hung in the air; a primal combination of musk and adrenaline that made the bear's fur stand on end. It watched as they slunk closer, their movements fluid and predatory, their eyes locked onto the sleeping man.

A deep rumble emanated from the bear's chest, a growl that shook the ground beneath its paws. Its eyes never wavered from the wolves, dark pools of intent that dared them to try to take what was not theirs. They circled around it, testing its patience with each step, but the bear remained still. This was a standoff, an ancient dance between apex predators.

The wolves sensed the tension in the air, a standoff between two apex predators. But while they desired the man, they were aware they would not be able to take him without first dealing with the bear's wrath. And so, one by one, they slinked away into the night, their tails tucked between their legs.

As silence settled over the forest once more, the bear let out a low snarl, a declaration that this was its territory and its responsibility to protect. It would stay vigilant throughout the night, understanding that the possibility of danger still lurked in every shadow.

The bear stood sentinel, its colossal frame towering over the sleeping man. The nocturnal world around them remained alive with a symphony of sounds, but the bear's senses were on high alert, every rustle and snap meticulously analysed. The wolves may have retreated for now, but the wilds were unpredictable, and the bear knew to never let its guard down.

The moon cast a silver glow, illuminating the man's peaceful face as he slept. But the bear regarded him with a mixture of curiosity and protectiveness, knowing that in this dangerous world, humans were fragile and needed watching over.

Time seemed to stretch on indefinitely, marked only by the slow arc of the moon across the sky. The bear shifted its weight from time to time, its paws firmly pressing into the earth with a solid strength that spoke of unyielding dominance. Even the ground itself seemed to take comfort in the presence of this powerful creature.

In an instant, a faint rustling broke through the quiet, sharper and closer than any other sound in the forest. The bear's head snapped towards it, eyes narrowing in anticipation. But it wasn't the wolves this time. It was something smaller, more tentative–a lone fox drawn by curiosity and the scent of potential scavenging.

For a brief moment, the fox met the bear's intense gaze before wisely retreating back into the underbrush. The tension in the bear's muscles eased slightly as it snorted in a quiet manner of dismissal. This was its realm, where even the boldest of creatures thought twice before challenging its authority.

As the first light of dawn began to filter through the trees, there was a shift in the air. The man stirred again, blinking away sleep as he sat up slowly. His gaze met with the bear's once more, and there was a silent understanding between them–a recognition of each other's place in this harsh world filled with danger at every turn.

FINNIAN

One afternoon, Finnian found himself caught in a gentle rain. He stood beneath the canopy of trees, listening to the soothing patter of raindrops on leaves. The air was filled with the fresh, earthy scent of rain. He closed his eyes, letting the cool drops wash over him.

The rain fell steadily, each droplet a tiny tap on the leaves above, creating a symphony of nature's own making. Finnian stood still, feeling the cool water trickle down his face, mingling with the warm tears he didn't realise he'd been shedding. It was a cleansing moment, a rare instance where the external world mirrored his internal turmoil.

As the minutes passed, the rain began to intensify, drumming louder on the forest canopy. Finnian opened his eyes, watching as the forest transformed around him. The leaves glistened with moisture, the ground beneath his feet turned soft and muddy, and the air seemed to hum with renewed life.

He tilted his head back, letting the rain wash away the dust and grime of countless days spent alone in the forest. For the first time in a long while, a connection to something larger than himself washed over him.

He breathed deeply, enjoying the fresh, earthy scent that only rain could bring. It filled his lungs and seemed to cleanse his soul. He could hear the distant call of a bird, its song blending harmoniously with the rhythm of the rain. It was as if the forest was singing a lullaby, soothing his weary spirit.

Suddenly, the rain began to turn colder and heavier. The gentle patter was replaced by the sharp sting of hailstones. Finnian looked up, alarmed, as the sky darkened and the hail intensified, bouncing off the ground and leaves with a force that shook the trees. Just then, he noticed a torrent of water cascading down from the mountain, heading straight for his shelter.

Panic surged through him as he sprinted toward his shelter to collect his pack before it collapsed under the weight of the rushing water. The structure that had once provided safety and solace was swept away in an instant. Finnian's heart pounded in his chest as he realised, he needed to find a new refuge, and fast.

Upon seeing a cave in the distance, he hurried towards it, his feet sliding in the rapidly forming mud. The hail pelted down, stinging his skin and driving him forward with urgent speed. The sound of the water crashing through the forest was deafening, and the ground trembled beneath him.

He reached the cave just as the torrent of water surged past his former shelter, the force of nature overwhelming everything in its path. Panting and soaked, Finnian ducked inside the cave, finding a rough, stony sanctuary. He collapsed against the cool, damp walls; his breaths ragged as he tried to steady himself.

The cave was dark and musty, but it was mostly dry and offered a sense of security. As the storm raged on outside, Finnian listened to the relentless pounding of the hail and the roar of the water. In the cave's embrace, relief washed over him. The storm's fury was a glaring reminder of nature's power, but within this new refuge, he found a small measure of safety.

He rummaged through his pack, tearing open the first aid kid. He wrapped himself in a foil blanket, huddling in the depths of the cave, sensing the warmth slowly return to his chilled body. The storm outside showed no signs of letting up, but Finnian knew that it, too, would eventually pass. In the aftermath, he would face the challenges of rebuilding, but for now, he allowed himself to rest, grateful for the shelter that protected him from the storm's wrath.

As the rain continued to pelt, Finnian was thankful for the foil blanket he had managed to salvage from the wreckage. The thought of trying to build a fire inside the cave amidst the storm seemed impossible. He was grateful for the simple invention and avoided catching his death.

Finnian huddled deeper into the blanket, trying to find respite from both the raging storm outside and the storm of emotions inside. A significant memory kept replaying in his mind, tormenting him with its sharp edges. He had been in prison for eight long months. The phone call from Igrit, John's mother, was like a knife twisting in his gut. Her words, full of sorrow and pain, echoed through the darkness. "John's gone, Finnian."

He felt his heart drop, the walls of the cave closing in on him as if to suffocate him. "What happened? What... what killed him?"

"It was pneumonia," Igrit answered, her voice trembling with grief. "He passed away in the hospital, with me by his side."

The storm continued to roar outside as Finnian was lost in his own internal tempest. He imagined John lying alone in a sterile hospital room, surrounded by beeping machines and the smell of disinfectant. The image of his friend's struggle and suffering weighed heavily on his soul. But among it all, he found a small succour in knowing that John had not been alone. His mother had been there for him until the very end. And yet, even that small comfort couldn't ease the burden of guilt and regret that consumed Finnian.

The cave offered shelter from the external storm, but nothing could shield him from the turmoil within. He could feel the weight of his emotions pressing down on him, threatening to drown him in a sea of despair. The sound of the hail and rain outside mirrored the chaos inside his mind, each icy drop a reminder of the pain he couldn't escape.

Hours seemed to pass in a blur of anguish. Finnian's thoughts spiralled, replaying the countless what-ifs and could-have-been. The memory of John's laughter, his unwavering support, and the bond they shared became a haunting chorus, echoing through the cavernous space of the cave.

In the quiet moments that followed, Finnian allowed himself to remember John in happier times. He recalled the adventures they had, the camaraderie that had defined their friendship. As the memories surfaced, they brought with them a bittersweet sense of closure. He knew John would want him to find peace, to heal, and to live on. Eventually, Finnian's exhaustion overcame him. He welcomed the deepest of sleep.

He dreamt of the night of the accident, his subconscious drifting back to that night while the deluge continued outside the cave. The images played out vividly in his mind. The rain-soaked road, the cyclist swerving into his path, the horrific crash that followed. He could almost feel the icy water filling his car, hear the muffled screams of the mother and her son. The guilt and terror of that night clung to him like a shroud.

THE BEAR

The bear had been fishing by the river, its powerful claws scooping up glistening, wriggling fish from the icy water. It revelled in the simple pleasure of the hunt, each successful catch a tribute to its skill and strength. The river's flow was steady and rhythmic, a constant companion to the bear's solitary existence. Upon standing on the cold, slated riverbank, the bear sensed a subtle shift in the air. The scent of damp earth tickled its nose, a prelude to the approaching storm. Moments later, the bear heard the distant rumble of thunder, a low growl that seemed to echo through the mountains. It sensed the vibrations beneath its feet, a tremor that communicated the storm's imminent arrival.

Instinct took over, and the bear abandoned its hunt, the fish forgotten in the face of nature's fury. It moved with purpose, muscles rippling beneath its thick fur as it raced through the forest. The canopy above rustled with the first whispers of the wind, leaves dancing in anticipation of the tempest.

The bear focused solely on reaching the safety of its cave. The path was familiar, etched into its memory from countless journeys through the wilderness. The terrain shifted from soft forest floor to rocky ground as the bear approached the mountainside, its paws pounding a steady rhythm against the earth. The sky darkened, heavy clouds gathering like an ominous veil. The rumble of thunder grew louder; the storm's obstinate advance. The bear pushed on, its breath coming in measured huffs as it navigated the twisting trails.

Finally, the entrance to its cave loomed ahead, a dark maw in the mountainside. The bear didn't slow until it was safely within the cavern's embrace, the cool, damp air a welcome refuge from the brewing chaos outside.

The bear paused abruptly. It was not alone.

GRACE

Grace paced back and forth in the living room, her feet leaving imprints on the plush carpet as she struggled to contain her roiling emotions. Her heart was like a stormy sea, waves of hurt and fear crashing against each other with every step she took. Meanwhile, Patrick sat stoically in his armchair, his face an unreadable mask that betrayed none of the turmoil he was going through inside. The silence between them was suffocating, stretching on for months and weighing heavily on their marriage.

With a trembling voice and tears welling up in her eyes, Grace finally broke the tense stillness. "Patrick," she began, her voice quivering with emotion, "I can't keep pretending everything is going to be okay. It's been five months, and we still have no answers."

Though she looked directly at him, Patrick's expression remained unchanged.

Frustration and anger boiled over in Grace, her fists clenching at her sides. "I'm losing my mind," she cried out.

"Every day that goes by with no news, I fear the worst. What if he's... what if he's dead? What if we never see our son again?"

She glared at her husband, willing him to show some sign of emotion. But he sat silently in his chair.

"Look at me!" she spat, desperation lacing her words, "Look at me and tell me you care about our son. Tell me you're afraid too. I need to know that you still care." As the last words escaped her lips, Grace crumpled to the ground in sobs. For a moment, Patrick stood and met her gaze with raw pain in his eyes.

"Of course I care," he whispered before turning and leaving the room, leaving Grace alone on the floor of their living room, consumed by grief.

FINNIAN

A sudden, guttural growl shattered his reverie. Finnian's eyes snapped open, his breath catching in his throat. At the entrance of the cave stood the bear, its massive form silhouetted against the morning light. The bear's eyes gleamed with a fierce intensity, its growls reverberating through the cave like rolling thunder.

Finnian's heart pounded in his chest, the primal fear of facing such a powerful predator surging through him. The bear pawed at the dirt, its movements agitated and forceful. It was clear that the cave was its territory, and it was not pleased with the intruder.

The bear advanced, its growls growing louder, more insistent. Finnian was paralysed with fear, every instinct screaming at him to flee, but his body wouldn't obey. The bear's powerful slaps against the ground sent vibrations through the cave, a tangible manifestation of its displeasure.

As the bear drew closer, Finnian's mind raced. He had to get out; had to escape. Summoning every ounce of courage, he slowly began to move, inching towards the entrance. The bear watched him, its eyes never leaving his form, a mix of curiosity and warning in its gaze.

With a final, thunderous growl, the bear backed away just enough for Finnian to make his move. He scrambled out of the cave, his heart hammering in his chest. Once outside, he turned to see the bear standing at the entrance, facing toward the back of the cage. It pawed at the ground, its claws digging into the dirt, asserting its dominance.

With a surge of primal urgency, the bear lunged into the cave, disappearing into the darkness. Finnian stood outside, heart still pounding from the encounter. Suddenly, a rustle and growling echoed from within. He strained to see, a mix of fear and curiosity rooting him to the spot.

Moments later, the bear emerged, a rattlesnake clamped in its powerful jaws. It shook its head vigorously, slapping the snake around. Finnian stood stiff and stunned, unable to tear his eyes away from the scene. The bear's raw power was both terrifying and mesmerizing.

With a final, decisive motion, the bear threw the snake into the dirt, thumping it with its paws until it lay still, lifeless.

The bear huffed, sitting in the entrance of the cave to rest from its exertion.

Finnian glanced at the bear, the initial terror slowly ebbing away. The bear's presence was oddly comforting, a reminder of the delicate balance between nature's fury and its unexpected moments of grace.

BAREE

Baree trudged up the familiar path to Leif residence, each step weighed down by the crushing weight of worry that had plagued her for months. She had made this journey countless times, desperate for any news or sign. Clutching the contact information like a lifeline, she approached the door and knocked softly, her heart pounding with anticipation.

The door creaked open to reveal Finnian's mother, her eyes filled with the same torment and anguish that Baree felt. "Baree, come in," she exhaled, making way for her to enter.

Despite the warm and welcoming atmosphere of the house, there was an undeniable tension in the air. They settled into the living room, their silent fears suffocating them as they waited for answers.

"Have you heard anything?" Baree asked in a barely audible whisper. Finnian's mother shook her head; her face etched with sorrow. "No, nothing. It has been six long months and still no trace of him. I fear we are running out of time."

Baree couldn't contain her frustration any longer. "I am enraged by the lack of effort from the emergency services. It's as if they have given up on Finnian." Tears welled up in Grace's eyes. "I know...they keep telling me they are doing everything they can, but it never feels enough. We are left in the dark, clinging to hope for any shred of information."

With tears streaming down her face, Baree reached out and took her hand, a symbol of their shared pain and ambition. "We cannot give up. We must continue to fight for him, to search for answers. He is out there somewhere, and he needs us."

A spark ignited in Grace's eyes, a glimmer of perseverance cutting through the sombre atmosphere. "You're right. We can't give up. We will keep searching, keep demanding answers. Finnian deserves that."

They sat together in the stillness of the living room, their resolve unbreakable. The journey ahead was daunting and uncertain, but they would face it together, united by their love for Finnian. They refused to succumb to the frustration and despair, determined to find him and bring him home.

FINNIAN

The forest path to the plane wreck was now a familiar one. Finnian navigated the terrain with a sense of dedication, his breath steady as he approached the twisted metal remnants of his crash. The once intimidating sight had become a source of potential, a treasure trove of survival tools.

As he reached the wreckage, Finnian began to sift through the debris, his hands moving with purpose. Most of the useful items had already been scavenged, but he continued searching, hopeful for any overlooked resources. The sun's rays filtered through the trees, casting patches of light on the broken pieces of the plane.

His fingers brushed against something hard and cold, half-buried under a pile of scattered belongings. Finnian pulled it free, revealing a small, weathered tin box. Curious, he pried it open. Inside, nestled amongst a few personal items, was a small souvenir, a miniature wooden bear.

He turned the bear over in his hands, a soft smile tugging at his lips. The carving was simple yet detailed, a symbol of strength and resilience. It felt like a serendipitous find, a reminder of his unlikely guardian in the forest.

Finnian placed the wooden bear in his pocket, feeling a transformed sense of connection to his journey. He continued to search the wreckage, but nothing else held the same significance as the small souvenir. With the sun beginning its descent, he decided it was time to head back to his camp.

As he walked through the forest, the wooden bear a reassuring presence in his pocket, Finnian felt a spark of confidence. The souvenir was a symbol of his survival, a token of the unexpected bond he had formed with the wild. Each step back to camp was lighter, the forest's beauty surrounding him and the promise of resilience guiding his path.

The mountain trail was steep and treacherous, but Finnian had grown accustomed to navigating its rugged terrain. The air was crisp, the scent of pine mingling with the earthy aroma of the forest floor. He moved carefully; each step deliberate as he made his way down the slope.

But then, his foot slipped on a loose rock. Time seemed to slow as he lost his balance, his arms flailing in a desperate attempt to steady himself. The ground rushed up to meet him, and he tumbled down the mountainside, the world a blur of rocks and branches.

Pain exploded through his body as he hit the ground hard. The wooden bear in his pocket snapped, the sharp splinters piercing his side. He cried out, the agony of the impact mingling with the sharp sting of the wood embedded in his flesh. His wrist twisted unnaturally beneath him, and he felt a sickening snap as a bone broke. His finger, too, was bent at an odd angle, the pain radiating up his arm. Finnian lay there, gasping for breath, his body wracked with pain. The forest around him seemed to close in, the trees towering above like silent sentinels. He tried to move, but every attempt sent waves of agony through his side and arm. The splinters from the wooden bear dug deeper into his skin. He forced himself to take slow, measured breaths, trying to calm his racing heart. The pain was overwhelming, but he knew he couldn't stay there. Summoning every ounce of strength, he managed to sit up, his vision swimming.

The hair on the back of his neck stood on end as a howl resounded through the forest. In a frantic search for the bear, his protector against the wolves, black filled his eyes. His world plunged into darkness as the blackout took him. He lies still.

Unconscious. Alone.

Finnian felt a sharp yank at his feet, dragging him violently from his slumber. He was being pulled across the ground, the rough terrain scraping against his skin. Disoriented and terrified, he kicked and yelled, trying to free himself. The animal's strong and unyielding grip made its grunts almost inaudible over his panicked cries.

The surrounding forest seemed to come alive with sounds, the once comforting shadows now filled with ominous shapes. Howling wolves echoed through the trees, their cries reverberating through the night. Finnian's heart raced, his mind scrambling to comprehend what was happening. The grunts of the creature pulling him were familiar, almost like a sense of protection. Realisation gradually came over him despite the haze of fear. It was the bear. The animal's powerful jaws gripped his ankle, dragging him with across the forest floor. Pain surged up his side as the splintered totem dug its way further into his hip.

The howls of the wolves grew louder, closer, their cries slicing through the night. Finnian's panic began to shift to a dawning understanding. The bear was not attacking him; it was saving him. The grip tightened as the bear continued to pull him through the underbrush, every muscle in its massive body straining with the effort.

Finnian winced in pain as he clutched his wrist close to his body, the other by his side in an attempt to add some shred of comfort to his burning side.

Finally, the bear halted, releasing Finnian at the entrance of its cave. Finnian's heart still raced, his breaths coming in quick, shallow gasps. The bear positioned itself defensively between him and the howling predators, turning to face the direction they had come from.

The wolves appeared, their eyes glowing eerily in the darkness, their forms ghostly silhouettes against the night. The bear let out a series of ferocious growls, a sound that resonated with primal authority. Finnian vanished inside the cave, finding protection behind a large rock. The wolves hesitated, sensing the bear's dominance.

Time stood still as both sides assessed their opponent. And then, with a defiant snarl, the wolf backed down, conceding defeat to the mighty bear. The others followed suit, retreating into darkness as the bear watched them with wary eyes. The threat may have passed for now, but the bear remained vigilant, knowing that danger lurked in every shadow of the unforgiving wilderness. It settled back into its watchful stance, a silent guardian keeping order in the chaotic night.

The bear turned to look at him. There was a moment of stillness, a silent communication between man and beast, a recognition of the bond that had formed.

Finnian's fear melted into a deep sense of gratitude. He stood up slowly, his body trembling from the adrenaline. The bear huffed softly; a sound that felt almost reassuring. It turned and sat at the entrance of the cave. For the first time in six months, Finnian felt safe.

THE BEAR

The bear crouched low in the dense underbrush, its dark fur blending seamlessly with the shadows. Its keen eyes followed every movement of the struggling man by the stream. The stranger's gaunt frame and ragged clothing were clear signs of his desperation for food.

As the man waded into the icy water, his clumsy attempts to catch fish onehanded were met with failure time and again. The fish taunted him with their swift movements and clever evasions, while his frustration grew more palpable with each empty-handed reach. The lines of exhaustion on his face deepened, highlighting the toll that hunger and fatigue had taken on him.

The bear tilted its head in curiosity and empathy, a primal stirring within its heart as it watched the man's struggles. He shifted his position in the stream, trying different techniques in vain: scooping, grabbing, even attempting to pin the fish against rocks with one hand, the other positioned at his breast, motionless.

But nothing worked. The elusive creatures slipped through his fingers like water, mocking his desperation. His breath came in laboured gasps, each failure draining his strength and resolve. As he stumbled to the bank and collapsed onto the muddy ground, the full weight of his situation settled heavily on his shoulders. Silently and effortlessly, the bear moved through the foliage towards the stream. Its powerful paws made almost no sound despite its immense size. With one swift swipe of its massive paw, it scooped a fish from the water with ease.

The bear approached the man, holding out the fish with its nose and rolling it towards Finnian's head. The fish flopped against him, startling him awake from his exhausted stupor. His eyes widened in shock and confusion as he saw the imposing figure of the bear standing before him against the backdrop of the forest. For a moment, frozen in time, man and beast locked eyes. The bear's gaze was steady and unwavering, devoid of any malice. It watched as Finnian's initial fear slowly gave way to a tentative understanding. With deliberate movements, the bear backed away, its mission accomplished.

Finnian sat in awe and wonder, a single hand trembling as he reached out to take the fish from the bear. In that moment, he realised that survival in this wild place extended beyond the limits of his own strength.

The bear disappeared into the woods.

POACHERS

Winter was around the corner. Animals were scavenging to stock up before the air grew glacial. Before food grew scarce. The remaining few days of autumn brought about the last of its sunshine. Finnian sat in a sunlit clearing, the gentle rays of the sun warming his skin. The forest around him was alive with the sounds of birdsong and the rustle of leaves. Nearby, the bear lay basking in the sun, its great form relaxed and content. Finnian closed his eyes, savouring the moment of peace. The long, harsh winter was looming. He took a deep breath, the scent of the changing season invigorating his senses.

Finnian took out the book he salvaged from the plane and began reading in the sunlight. As he read through the passages, he couldn't help but chuckle at the thought. "You're like Gandalf," he murmured, looking toward the bear. "Never around when I want you, but always there when I need you." Finnian watched the bear as it basked in the sunlight, the creature's substantial form radiating a sense of serene power. A smile tugged at the corners of his mouth as he thought about naming the bear after the grey wizard.

A wizard is never late, nor is he early. He arrives precisely when he means to. He chuckled softly, the words resonating with the bear's uncanny knack for showing up just when Finnian needed it most.

The sunlight danced on the forest floor, creating a scene that was almost magical. In that moment, Finnian felt a deep sense of connection, not just to the bear, but to the wild world around them. Gandalf, in his own way, was more than a guardian; he was a reminder of the wonder and unpredictability of nature.

The sharp crack of a gunshot shattered the peace. Finnian's eyes snapped open, his heart pounding in his chest. The bear, too, reacted instantly, its ears pricking up and its body tensing. The sound of the gunshot echoed through the forest.

The bear sprang to its feet, its instincts taking over. With a powerful burst of speed, it raced into the forest, heading in the direction of its cave. Finnian watched in alarm as the bear disappeared into the trees, the urgency of its movements a clear sign of the threat.

Panic surged through Finnian as he realised the implications. Poachers were near, and the bear's safety was at risk. He knew he had to act quickly, to find a way to protect both himself and the bear. The clearing, once a haven of peace, had become a place of danger.

Finnian scrambled to his feet, his mind racing with possibilities. He needed to find a way to warn the bear, to keep it safe from the poachers' guns. The bond he had formed with the bear over the past months was strong, and he couldn't bear the thought of losing his unlikely guardian.

With his force of survival fuelling his every step, Finnian set off in the direction the bear had gone. The forest closed in around him; the shadows deepening as he moved deeper into the trees. The sound of his own breathing and the pounding of his heart were the only things he could hear.

As he ran, Finnian's thoughts were a whirlwind of fear and resolve. He had survived this far, forged a connection with the wild, and found a sense of purpose. Now, he would do whatever it took to protect the bear and ensure their survival. Finnian tore through the dense forest, his heart hammering in his chest as he tracked the bear's trail. The deafening echo of another gunshot reverberated in his ears. He knew he had to find the bear before the ruthless poachers did, or all would be lost.

As he drew nearer to where the gunshot had pierced the once peaceful forest, Finnian slowed his pace and stalked forward with caution, every sense heightened for any sign of danger. The usual chorus of wildlife had fallen silent, replaced by an eerie stillness that hung heavy in the air. He could feel the weight of impending peril bearing down on him.

Then he heard it, low, gruff voices murmuring in hushed tones. Finnian crept closer, his eyes darting around for any sign of where they might be coming from. He spotted two men, rifles slung over their shoulders, as they studied a map intently. They were mere yards away from where the bear was hiding behind a thick cluster of trees.

The bear's keen senses had also picked up on their presence and its muscles tensed, ready to defend itself at any moment. Finnian knew he had little time to act. With quick thinking, he grabbed a nearby rock and hurled it in the opposite direction, hoping to cause a diversion.

The rock landed with a loud thud, immediately catching the poachers' attention and causing them to turn their guns towards the noise. Taking advantage of their distraction,

Finnian swiftly moved closer to the bear and whispered soothing words to guide it away from harm.

The bear understood and followed his lead, moving slowly and silently as they made their way out of sight from the poachers. As they reached safety within the cave, Finnian breathed a sigh of relief but knew they couldn't let their guard down just yet. The forest was their sanctuary, but it was also a treacherous place. As the sun began to set, casting ominous shadows across the cave walls, Finnian's ambition only grew stronger. He would do whatever it took to protect himself and the bear from the constant threat that loomed in the darkness of the forest. They were survivors, warriors of the wild, and they would brave any danger that came their way.

THE PACK

The dense forest had fallen into a hush, the mournful silence settling over the trees like a shroud. But the wolves, ever vigilant and attuned to their surroundings, had not missed the sharp ring of the gunshot. The scent of humans and fear lingered in the air, setting their primal instincts on edge. The pack gathered, silent and focused, their senses honed by years of surviving in the harsh wilderness.

Leading the pack was a grizzled alpha with piercing eyes that seemed to see through the very core of one's being. Its movements were purposeful as it led its pack through the underbrush. Each member moved with calculated stealth, their bodies blending seamlessly into their surroundings. Following a fresh scent trail, they moved towards the poachers' camp.

As they neared the camp, the wolves spread out in a strategic formation, ready for any potential threats. The alpha paused for a moment, its acute sense of smell taking in every detail of its surroundings. The humans were unaware of their presence, too engrossed in their map and rifles.

The wolves closed in silently, their eyes glinting in the dim light. With a low growl from the alpha, the pack came to a halt. Their sharp teeth bared as they waited for further orders. The humans remained oblivious; their backs turned towards the advancing predators.

Suddenly, one poacher felt a prickling sensation at the back of his neck. Slowly turning around, his eyes widened in shock as he spotted the lead wolf standing before him. Its gaze was intense and unyielding, sending shivers down his spine. He nudged his companion frantically, pointing towards the circling pack.

"Look," he mouthed soundlessly. "Wolves."

The other poacher froze at the sight of multiple pairs of predatory eyes watching them from the shadows. His grip tightened on his rifle in a futile attempt to ward off the increasing sense of danger. But the alpha wolf issued a silent warning, its teeth bared in an imposing display.

Both poachers were well aware that they were no match for the pack of wolves, outnumbered and outmanoeuvred. A tense standoff ensued, with neither side making a move. The forest held its breath, waiting for the tension to break. With another menacing growl from the alpha, the pack inched closer towards the humans, their bodies coiled like springs ready to strike. Feeling the weight of their impending doom, the poachers slowly began to back away, their movements calculated and cautious. They knew that one wrong move could cause the wolves to attack. But their actions were not fast enough.

The first wolf ascended onto them. Followed by the second and the third. Tearing limbs and opening throats. the poachers screamed a gargled matinee of helpless pleas.

The alpha issued another low growl, conveying that they had accomplished their task. The animals left the lifeless, bloodied, disembodied remains of the poachers on the forest floor and slipped away through the trees.

HIKERS

Each step through the dense underbrush was a careful dance, their eyes scanning the forest floor for unstable ground. The rainforest loomed around them. They kept their voices low, the tranquillity of their surroundings lending an eerie calm to their chatter.

But as they turned a bend in the trail, the leading hiker froze in his tracks, his hand shooting up to signal the others. The forest seemed to hold its breath, the only sound the faint rustle of leaves in the breeze. He knelt down, his expression shifting from curiosity to terror.

"What is it?" one of his companions asked, her voice barely above a whisper as she joined him. And then she saw it too: scattered among the fallen leaves and moss were the remains of a campsite, torn fabric and scattered gear mingled with the skeletal remains of a human body. Bones lay strewn about like discarded scrap, some still coated in shreds of rotting flesh.

A chill ran down their spines as they stood frozen in horror, their hearts pounding so loudly they could hear them over the silence of the forest. They fumbled for their phones, their shaking fingers dialling for help as they reported the grisly scene before them. Trees towered above them like silent witnesses to this gruesome discovery, and as if on cue, a blood-curdling howl pierced through the stillness.

Without a word, all four hikers broke into a sprint, their feet pounding against the forest floor as they raced through tangled vines and thick foliage. The thought of what kind of creature could have done this drove them forward, fear pushing them faster and faster towards their only means of escape.

"Start the engine!" one of them shouted as they burst into the small clearing where their helicopter waited. Their voices came out in frantic gasps as they scrambled into the aircraft, their eyes wide with terror as they prepared for take-off.

The bright red and white helicopter stood out against the green backdrop of the forest, beckoning them with its promise of safety. But as they lifted off and flew over the rainforest, the fear and adrenaline still coursing through their veins, they couldn't shake the feeling that something sinister was watching them from below. And they knew they were lucky to have escaped with their lives.

GRACE

Finnian's parents sat together on the worn, comfortable couch in their living room, the soft hum of the television filling the space. Baree sat across from them, her fingers nervously twisting the fabric of her sweater. The atmosphere was heavy with unspoken worry, the uncertainty of Finnian's fate weighing on all of them.

The news anchor's voice cut through the silence, the usual drone of daily updates suddenly carrying a note of urgency. "Breaking news," she announced. "Hikers in a remote forest of British Columbia have discovered the remains of a male. Authorities are working to identify the body, but initial reports suggest the remains have been there for some time."

Finnian's mother gasped, her hand flying to her mouth as her eyes widened in shock. His father clenched his fists, the muscles in his jaw tightening as he tried to process the information. Baree felt her heart drop, a cold dread settling in her stomach. She leaned forward, her eyes fixed on the screen, hoping for more details.

The anchor continued, "The discovery was made earlier yesterday, and a team of investigators are currently on the scene. The identity of the deceased has not been confirmed; however, speculation would surmise that the remains may belong to missing man Finnian Leif. More updates to come."

Finnian's mother began to cry softly, tears streaming down her cheeks as she clutched her husband's hand. He squeezed back, his own eyes misty but determined to stay strong for her. Baree felt a lump form in her throat, her mind racing with a thousand thoughts and fears. Could it be Finnian? Had their worst fears come true?

As the news segment moved on to other stories, the room fell into a heavy silence. Finnian's parents held each other, their grief and anxiety palpable. Baree sat back; her mind numb with the possibility that the remains could be Finnian's. She had always held onto a sliver of hope that he was out there, surviving against the odds. Now, that optimism appeared fragile and tenuous.

"We need to go to the authorities," Grace finally spoke, her voice steady but laced with pain. "We need to find out if it's him."

PATRICK

Patrick stood at the threshold of Finnian's old bedroom, the door slightly ajar, as if inviting him into a world long past. With a deep breath, he stepped inside, the familiar scent of his son's childhood clinging to the air. The room was untouched, a sanctuary frozen in time. Posters of sports teams adorned the walls, and trophies, books, and mementos of happier days lined the shelves.

He ambled to the bed, the soft creak of the floorboards a gentle reminder of the many nights he had tucked Finnian in, reading him bedtime stories and whispering reassurances in the dark. Patrick lowered himself onto the bed, the mattress still firm beneath him, holding the weight of years gone by.

His eyes fell upon the photo on the side table, a snapshot of unadulterated joy. Finnian and John, both ten years old, stood side by side, their oversized baseball gloves almost comically large in their small hands. Their smiles were wide and toothy, filled with the innocence and exuberance of youth.

Patrick's heart ached as he reached out to pick up the photo, his fingers tracing the edges of the frame.

Tears welled up in his eyes, blurring the image of the two boys who had once been inseparable. The weight of loss and regret pressed down on him, the memories of Finnian's laughter and the sound of John's voice like distant echoes in the silence. Patrick clutched the photo to his chest, the dam of emotions breaking free as he began to sob uncontrollably.

The room, so silent and still, seemed to amplify his cries, each sob a painful cue of the time that had slipped away, the moments that could never be reclaimed. Patrick wept for the son he had lost to a future filled with heartache, for the friendship that tragedy had torn apart, and for the innocence that had been irrevocably shattered. He also wept for John, who had been like a second son to him. Patrick missed the boy's infectious energy and the bond he shared with Finnian.

In the quiet of Finnian's childhood bedroom, surrounded by the remnants of a life once full of promise, Patrick allowed himself to grieve. His tears fell onto the bedspread, soaking into the fabric like the unspoken words and unresolved feelings that weighed heavily on his heart. The photo remained clutched in his hand, a fragile connection to a past that felt both near and impossibly distant. As the sobs subsided into quiet sniffles, Patrick lay back on the bed, staring up at the ceiling. The room seemed to hold him in a gentle embrace, offering a moment of solace amid the storm of his emotions. He knew he couldn't change the past, but in that moment, he allowed himself to mourn, to feel the full depth of his sorrow.

The minutes stretched on, and Patrick lay there, the silence of the room enveloping him like a comforting blanket. He knew he would have to leave eventually, to face the world outside and the challenges that awaited. But for now, he remained in Finnian's room, holding on to the memories, the pain, and the love that would forever bind him to his son and to John.

FINNIAN

Finnian watched as the bear began to prepare for hibernation, its massive form moving methodically as it readied its den for the long, cold months ahead. He knew that when the bear went into hibernation, he would be without his unlikely guardian. The wolves, ever watchful, would see him as fair game.

Determined to protect himself, Finnian turned to the wreckage of the plane with an idea forming in his mind. He began to dig a trench surrounding the aircraft; the earth yielding slowly to his efforts. As he worked, the plane seemed to sink deeper into the ground, a fortress taking shape within the wilderness. Finnian layered branches around the surface of the plane, each one placed with precision and care. He packed the gaps with moss and leaves, filling every hole and sealing every patch. The work was gruelling, but it kept his mind focused and his body warm against the encroaching chill.

He used mud to compact it all tightly, creating a barrier against the elements and any potential threats. The trench around the plane became a moat, an added layer of defence. As the sun dipped below the horizon, casting long shadows across his makeshift fortress, Finnian surveyed his work with a sense of accomplishment.

The aircraft, once a symbol of disaster, had become his shield against the wild. Finnian knew that winter would bring new challenges. He looked at his fortified shelter. It wasn't perfect, but it reflected his ingenuity.

As the first stars twinkled in the night sky, Finnian settled inside the plane, the wooden bear still in his pocket. The forest around him grew quiet, the nocturnal creatures beginning their nightly routines. He listened to the sounds, feeling a sense of connection to the wild, even as he sought to protect himself from its dangers.

With his preparations complete, Finnian allowed himself a moment of rest. He knew the coming months would be tough, but he was ready to face them head-on. The bear's hibernation, the wolves' lurking presence, the icy grasp of winter, all of it was a part of the journey. And Finnian was determined to survive.

Finnian's preparations for winter continued with a sense of urgency. The forest around him held the promise of sustenance, but it required diligence and resourcefulness to unearth its hidden treasures. Each day, he set out with a woven basket in hand, determined to gather enough food to see him through the harsh months ahead.

He foraged for berries, searching the underbrush for clusters of dark, juicy fruit. The berries were a sweet find, a welcome addition to his winter stores. Finnian moved with purpose, plucking each one carefully to avoid damaging the plants. His fingers, stained with berry juice, worked swiftly as he filled his basket. Barks and grubs were next on his list. Finnian had learned which trees provided the best edible bark and which logs harboured nutritious grubs. He stripped the bark from the trees with practiced efficiency, rolling it into tight bundles for drying. Digging through decaying wood, he extracted wriggling grubs, their protein-rich bodies a crucial component of his winter diet.

Small animals were harder to come by, but Finnian's patience paid off. He set traps and snares, checking them regularly. On good days, he caught rabbits or squirrels, their meat a precious resource. He carefully dried the meat, hanging strips over a small fire to preserve them.

As he gathered and processed his finds, Finnian stored everything in the plane. The aircraft, now fortified and weatherproofed, served as a makeshift pantry. He arranged the dried meat in neat rows, stacked bundles of bark, and placed baskets of berries and grubs in cool, shaded corners. Each item had its place organised and accessible.

The days grew shorter, and the chill in the air deepened. Finnian's wrist ached constantly, a dull reminder of his vulnerability. But he pushed through the pain, driven by the need to survive. His efforts were paying off, the plane was filling with provisions, showcasing his fortitude and adaptability.

Finnian took a moment to survey his work, a small sense of pride warming him against the cold. He knew that winter would be a test.

BAREE

The search and rescue helicopter soared over the vast expanse of the rainforest, its rotors slicing through the crisp winter air. Below, the forest stretched out in an endless sea of green, now blanketed in a thick layer of snow. The team inside scanned the landscape with trained eyes, looking for any sign of the missing aircraft.

The lead rescuer adjusted the binoculars, focusing on the dense canopy and the winding rivers snaking through the forest. The mission was a desperate one; finding any trace of Finnian Leif's plane amidst the unforgiving wilderness. The snow-covered trees made the search even more challenging, each mound of white blending seamlessly with the next.

"Anything yet?" the pilot asked, his voice crackling over the intercom. "Not so far," the lead rescuer replied, his tone heavy with frustration. "Just trees and more trees."

Baree sat tensely beside them, her eyes scanning the forest below. Her heart ached with worry for Finnian, and every moment that passed without a sign of him deepened her anxiety.

As they approached the coastline, the helicopter banked sharply, revealing a narrow strip of rocky beach. In the rugged terrain, something caught the lead rescuer's eye. "Hold on, what's that down there?"

The pilot adjusted their course, bringing the helicopter lower. The team peered out the windows, spotting a small boat stranded on the shoreline. It stood out starkly against the snowy backdrop, its weathered hull partially buried in the sand.

"That's no aircraft," one of the rescuers remarked, "but it looks like it's been there a while."

The lead rescuer nodded, snapping a few photos with his camera. "Let's get a closer look."

The helicopter hovered over the coastline as the team examined the boat from above. It was clear that the vessel had been abandoned for some time. Debris scattered around it suggested it had belonged to the poachers.

"Could be connected to the poachers we've been hearing about," the pilot suggested. "But no sign of a plane."

The lead rescuer sighed, the weight of the situation pressing down on him. "If he's down there, surviving the winter in these conditions… it would be a miracle."

Baree's eyes filled with tears as she listened to their words. The reality of Finnian's situation hit her hard, but she refused to give up. She leaned forward, gripping the edge of her seat. "We have to keep looking. He's out there, and he's strong. He'll find a way."

"You'll have to wait until Spring. Winter lasts through February. During this time, the temperature drops significantly, and the region experiences high levels of precipitation, including rain and snow, especially in higher elevations. The days become shorter, and the forest transforms into a wintry wonderland, presenting additional challenges. It's too risky."

The team shared a grim silence as the helicopter ascended once more, continuing its search over the snow-covered forest. Each passing minute felt like an eternity. The expanse of the wilderness was a gesture of the fragility of life in such an unforgiving place. The promise of finding Finnian alive dwindled with every sweep of the terrain, but the search pressed on, driven by the faint glimmer of hope that he might still be out there, fighting to survive.

GRACE

The television buzzed with urgent news, the anchor's voice carrying a heavy weight as she spoke. "Authorities have confirmed that the remains found do not belong to the missing man, Finnian Leif. Recent autopsy results report that two separate DNA results have been found among the remains. Confirming there was more than one individual found in the remote forest. The identity of the individuals is still unknown. The search for Finnian Leif continues."

The relief that washed over the Leif household was immediate, but it was quickly replaced by a sense of urgency. The living room was suddenly alive with the incessant ringing of phones and the buzzing of alerts. Grace's house phone rang off the hook; each call another wave of concern and curiosity. Her mobile, lying on the coffee table, buzzed with a flurry of notifications; messages, calls, and alerts from friends and family members seeking information about the latest news report. Grace's hands shook as she picked up her mobile, her eyes darting across the screen as messages poured in.

"Grace, we just caught up with the news. Is it true?"

"Please do not hesitate to reach out if you need anything."

"Have they found Finnian? What's going on?"

Patrick remained in his armchair, frustration forming at his brow. Grace tried to compose herself, taking a deep breath as she answered a call.

"Hello?"

"Grace, it's Linda. We saw the news. Is it Finnian? Did they find him?"

Grace swallowed hard, her voice trembling. "No, Linda. The remains... they're not Finnian's. But they found a boat on the coastline of British Columbia. The autopsy showed two separate DNA results, confirming there were two individuals who lost their lives."

"Oh, Grace, I can't imagine what you're going through. Please, keep us informed if there's anything we can do to assist.

"I will, Linda. Thank you," Grace replied, her voice cracking with emotion. As she hung up, the phone immediately rang again. She understood that the calls were motivated by love and concern. After answering each one with as much composure as she could muster, she repeated the same information, experiencing the same heartache with every word.

Patrick, unable to bear the tension any longer, grabbed his coat and brushed past Grace, out the front door.

"Patrick, where are you going?" Grace called after him, her voice tinged with worry and confusion.

PATRICK

Patrick embodied the image of a man of few words, often mistaken for cold or indifferent. His silence was a fortress, impenetrable and stoic. It seemed as if he didn't care about Finnian or the devastating loss of John. But beneath the hard exterior lay a heart weighed down by sorrow and unspoken pain.

Raised in an era and environment where emotions were considered a weakness, Patrick learned early on to repress his feelings, to bury them deep within. He grew into a hard man, influenced by the expectation of being strong and unyielding. This stoicism served him well in many aspects of life, but it left him isolated in moments of profound grief.

John's death had struck him deeply, carving a wound that had never truly healed. John was like a son to him, his laughter and energy a cherished part of Patrick's world. The heavy burden of loss weighed heavily on Patrick, causing his heart to break a little more each day as he carried it silently.

The heartbreak extended to his relationship with Finnian. Patrick longed to open up and bridge the chasm that grew between them. He was acutely aware of Finnian's struggles, the hardships his son had endured. His sadness regarding Finnian remained a constant ache, a wound festering beneath the surface. He yearned to offer comfort, to share the weight of the pain, but the words never came.

Patrick's silence often gave the impression of indifference. However, it actually resulted from a lifetime of learned restraint. His heart ached for his son, empathizing with everything Finnian experienced. Every fibre of his being wanted to reach out, to hold him close and offer succour. But the lifelong habits proved difficult to change, and Patrick stayed ensnared in the cage he had constructed for himself.

His heart, though hardened by years of repression, beat with a deep, unspoken love for Finnian. Patrick experienced a silent struggle, a battle waged within the confines of his soul. His love and pain remained hidden beneath the surface, disguised by the tough exterior that became his shield. But they were there, undeniable and enduring, waiting for the moment when he could finally find the courage to let them show.

FINNIAN

Finnian barricaded himself inside the plane, the cold metal walls now a fortress against the brutal winter storm. He had painstakingly reinforced every inch of the wreckage, determined to make it his home for the long, cruel months ahead. The snow came in a merciless onslaught, burying the forest in a thick blanket of white.

The plane was now entombed under several metres of snow; an avalanche having mercilessly cascaded over it. The small entrance Finnian had carved out was his only lifeline, a narrow tunnel connecting him to the outside world.

Inside, the air was frigid and still, the howling of wolves in the distance a constant reminder of his vulnerability. Finnian huddled beneath his foil blanket, trying to block out the chilling emptiness around him.

He reached for his meagre rations, picking through a mix of berries, dried meat, roots, and bark. Each bite was a struggle, but he forced himself to eat, knowing that it was his only chance of survival. The flavours were a jumble of sweetness, saltiness, and bitterness, but they sustained him with their precious nourishment.

Finnian attempted to read his book by the dim light filtering through the cracks in the wreckage. But the pages blurred before his tired eyes, frustration mounting as he struggled to lose himself in the story. Eventually, he gave up and closed the book, unable to continue in such impossible conditions.

Days bled into nights as Finnian retreated deeper into his self-made prison. The passing of time marked only by the haunting sounds of predators lurking just beyond his fragile shelter. Yet even in this desolate place, Finnian clung to hope. He had survived this long, and he refused to give up now. His will to live burned bright despite the never-ending darkness that surrounded him.

As he settled in for another restless night, the distant howls of the wolves resounded through the forest. Solitude weighed heavily on him, the deafening silence of the snow-covered forest a cruel reminder of just how alone he was. On a brutally frigid night, the wind howled like a savage creature outside, its biting chill creeping into his makeshift shelter. Finnian curled up under the thin foil blanket for warmth and closed his eyes, hoping to find some relief in sleep. But as always, memories of home and loved ones tormented him, serving as a bitter reminder of what he had left behind. He couldn't help but think about the bear. However, painful flashbacks continued to plague his mind; the accident, John's illness and eventual passing, and his release from prison all resurfaced in his thoughts.

Finnian sat in the cold and dingy cell, feeling the weight of the world crushing down on him. The trial had been brutal. Every detail of the accident picked apart and analysed. He had tried to defend himself, but the overwhelming guilt consumed him as he relived that night. Two lives lost because of his own reckless decisions.

The sentence was delivered: five to seven years in prison for DUI, resulting in vehicular manslaughter. It felt like a death sentence, a punishment that seemed far too harsh for his actions. For two long years, Finnian served his time, each day dragging on with no end in sight. But then, fresh evidence emerged; a witness who saw everything that happened. The pizza delivery cyclist, not Finnian, was responsible for the accident. The cyclist had swerved into the road, causing Finnian's car to crash into another vehicle. A belated confession also came to light, supporting the recently discovered evidence.

During the hearing, the truth finally came to light. The court declared Finnian innocent, and he was exonerated. The taste of freedom was both sweet and bitter. Yes, he was no longer a prisoner, but the scars of his wrongful conviction would never truly disappear.

As he walked out of the courtroom, Finnian couldn't shake off the lingering shadows of his past. The warm sunlight hit his face as he stepped outside of the prison gates and took a deep breath. The future ahead was uncertain and daunting, but he was determined to move forward and make amends for his mistakes. The world looked different now, filled with both challenges and opportunities for redemption. With each step he took, Finnian carried the lessons from his journey
- a reminder of resilience and the enduring hope for a better tomorrow.

In the dead of night, Finnian's eyes shot open at the sound of rhythmic tapping. Panic flooded through him as he strained to listen. Something or someone was scratching at his shelter's entrance, eager to break in. With shaking hands, Finnian grabbed his makeshift spear and prepared for battle.

As the tapping grew louder and more persistent, Finnian steeled himself for whatever came next. The forest may have thrown countless challenges his way, but he refused to back down. He had faced the wolves, conquered the bitter cold, and endured unbearable isolation. And now he would fight with everything he had to protect what little semblance of safety he had created.

BAREE

Baree sat in the corner of a quaint cafe, sunlight filtering through the windows, casting a warm glow on the rustic wooden table. She absently stirred her iced tea, lost in thought, while her friends chatted animatedly around her. Their laughter and conversation provided a comforting background hum until a familiar name pierced through the din.

"Finnian Leif," one of her friends, Pierce, said with a scoff. "Heard they're still searching the forest for him. Honestly, no one could survive out there this long. I think he's dead."

"Yeah, how can we be sure he is in that forest?" chimed in Blake, her voice dripping with disdain. "That place is enormous. He could be anywhere, or nowhere."

"Maybe he doesn't deserve to survive," another friend interjected, her tone just as cold.

"Remember, people say he was driving drunk and crashed into that family's car? They say he killed them all."

"Most likely got what he deserved."

166

Baree felt her chest tighten. Her fingers gripped the edge of the table as she struggled to process their words. None of them were aware that she had been seeing Finnian before he disappeared. There wasn't a person among them who was acquainted with the Finnian she was familiar with. The kind and gentle soul she had developed feelings for was in such contrast to the man they mentioned with such bitterness.

A mixture of anger, sadness, and guilt churned within her. She wanted to defend him, to inform them that they were not aware of the complete story. But could she? Would it even matter? She bit her lip, swallowing the urge to speak out.

She was unable to remain seated and continue listening any further. The room felt suffocating, and the weight of their judgment pressed down on her. She stood abruptly, her chair scraping loudly against the floor.

She whispered almost silently, "I need some air."

As she stepped outside, the cool breeze hit her face, offering a small measure of relief. She walked away, each step taking her further from the judgment and closer to the solitude she needed desperately to sort through her conflicted emotions.

FINNIAN

As Spring arrived, weeks blurred into months as the relentless struggle to survive consumed Finnian's days. The once smooth skin of his hands now bore rough calluses from endless hours of building and foraging.

Finnian stalked through the forest, senses on high alert as he searched for sustenance. The air was thick with tension, each step causing the underbrush to snap like a gunshot beneath his boots. Every muscle in his body was coiled, ready to spring into action at the slightest hint of movement.

As he scoured for food, a sense of unease prickled at the back of Finnian's mind. The usual symphony of wildlife sounds was eerily absent, replaced by an unnerving silence that made his skin crawl. Suddenly, a low growl pierced the stillness, followed by the rustle of leaves. He turned just in time to see a pack of wolves emerge from the shadows, their eyes gleaming with hunger and malice. The lead wolf bared its teeth in a menacing snarl, signalling the start of the hunt. Adrenaline surged through Finnian's veins as he clutched his crude spear, knowing that he was no match for these predators without his bear companion by his side.

With no sign of the bear, Finnian knew he had to defend himself against the pack alone. He shouted a fierce battle cry as he lunged at the nearest wolf, thrusting his makeshift weapon forward with all his might. The wolf yelped and retreated momentarily, but its pack mates were quick to fill in the gap, snarling and snapping at Finnian with razor-sharp teeth.

With each passing second, Finnian's strength dwindled as he fought off vicious attack after attack. One wolf managed to sink its teeth into his leg, drawing blood and sending waves of searing pain through him. But he refused to back down, fuelled by sheer desire and survival instincts.

Just when it seemed like Finnian couldn't hold out any longer, a deafening roar shook the forest. The grey had arrived just in time to save his human companion from certain death. The massive bear charged into the fray, scattering the wolves with its sheer size and ferocity.

As the pack retreated, whimpering in defeat, the bear stood protectively over Finnian, growling a warning to ensure their safety.

Finnian collapsed to his knees, gasping for air as he stared up at the towering form of the bear. Gratitude and awe filled his eyes as he realised that once again, the bear had saved him from certain death.

As the forest slowly returned to its natural rhythm, Finnian struggled to his feet, his leg throbbing with wounds, but his motivation was unshaken. He owed his life to the bear.

The adrenaline still coursed through his veins as he limped back to his shelter. The bear paced alongside him. The quiet of the forest seemed almost surreal after the chaos of the fight. The wind whispered through the trees, offering a moment of respite before the harsh reality set in again.

Reaching the wreckage that serves as his winter refuge, Finnian tended to his wounds with shaking hands and gritted teeth. The bear watched over him.

Finnian dashed through the dense forest, his eyes searching frantically for any helpful items to assist him in his quest. He had to cross the treacherous river before nightfall, and swimming was not an option. The water's icy chill and raging current might easily engulf him entirely. But Finnian was determined to survive.

His heart raced as he searched for materials, quickly selecting hefty logs and sturdy branches that were able to withstand the force of the river. With nimble fingers, he lashed them together with vines collected earlier, each knot pulled tight with a sense of urgency. The sun began to dip below the treetops, casting ominous shadows as he worked feverishly.

In the distance, the bear watched his every move with dark, unblinking eyes. Finnian paid it no mind, having grown accustomed to its presence in the wild. But today, the bear seemed different, almost on edge.

As dusk settled over the land, Finnian stepped back to admire his crude raft. It may not be perfect, but it would have to do. With the bear silently trailing behind him, he pushed the raft into the churning waters and climbed aboard.

The river welcomed him with a violent surge, its currents stronger and rapids fiercer than he had anticipated. The logs shuddered and groaned under the force of the water, threatening to break apart at any moment. Finnian braced himself against the makeshift paddles, desperately trying to steer against the powerful currents that seemed determined to throw him off course. As he battled against nature itself, a sense of dread filled him. This was not going to be an easy journey across the river.

The raft splintered in a violent explosion of wood and vines, sending Finnian tumbling into the frigid water. Panic gripped him as he struggled to keep his head above the churning current, the shattered remnants of the raft scattering around him like broken bones.

With each gasping breath, Finnian felt himself being dragged further downstream, the river's icy grip tightening around him. Desperate to escape, he kicked and flailed, but the relentless force of the water threatened to swallow him whole.

Just as he sensed his strength dwindling and his body sinking under, a powerful grip latched onto his collar. The bear had leapt into the water, its jaws clamping down on Finnian's shirt.

Together they fought against the merciless river, the bear's strength and tenacity pulling them towards shore. Finnian struggled to keep his eyes open, his limbs weighed down by exhaustion. He sensed the bear's unwavering support and protection. As they collapsed on the riverbank, their laboured breaths mingling with the sounds of rushing water and rustling leaves, Finnian looked up at the bear with both fear and gratitude in his heart. The bear met his gaze calmly, emitting a low growl that was both reassuring and commanding.

BAREE

Baree's heart was a heavy stone, dragging her down as she stumbled through the front door. The talk of Finnian still echoed in her mind, a constant barrage of doubts and fears that threatened to consume her. She barely registered Justin sitting on the couch, his eyes narrowing with suspicion as he saw her distressed state.

"Where have you been?" His voice sliced through the air like a knife, sharp and accusatory. "You look upset. Who were you with?"

Baree took a deep breath, trying to steady herself against the onslaught of questions. "I was with friends, Justin. I just... needed some space."

But Justin was already on his feet, his jealousy flaring into full-blown rage.

"Space? Or time with someone else? You think I don't know what's going on?" Her fists clenched at her sides; Baree felt the familiar knot of fear tighten in her chest. "Justin, this has nothing to do with you. We're divorced. I'm not sure why you care." She turned to leave, but he grabbed her arm with an iron grip.

"You're not going anywhere," he growled.

In an instant, Baree's own fury boiled over, fuelled by years of abuse and control at the hands of Justin. With a snarl of defiance, she pushed him away and made a break for the door.

But he caught up to her, his fist connecting with her face and sending her tumbling to the ground. Ignoring the pain coursing through her body, Baree climbed back to her feet and tried to make another escape.

Justin hadn't finished. He lunged at her again, slamming her into the wooden railing of the staircase. Splintered wood flew everywhere as she crashed to the floor in a pool of blood from where her head had hit the railing.

As she lay there, dazed and disoriented, Justin loomed over her.

"You're never leaving," he sneered, his face twisted into a sinister mask of control.

But Baree had finally reached her breaking point. A surge of raw, primal rage coursed through her body, giving her the strength to fight back. She grabbed a jagged piece of wood from the wreckage on the floor and plunged it into Justin's leg with all her might.

He howled in pain and stumbled backwards, giving Baree the opportunity she needed to escape. She rose to her feet and pushed him hard against the open front door, the shard still clutched tightly in her hand and pressed against his throat.

"I would rather die than stay with you," she growled into his ear with venomous conviction.

With one final push, she sent him sprawling out onto the porch as she made her escape. The cool evening air hit her face like a wave of freedom, a mix of fear and liberation swimming through her as she left behind the toxic environment for good.

FINNIAN

Finnian's patience had begun to wear thin. The days blurred into weeks, and the weeks into months of stagnant existence in the never-ending wilderness. His once strong sense of purpose was dwindling, overshadowed by a growing sense of desperation.

The wreckage of the plane taunted him daily, a constant reminder of his isolation and helplessness. He took out his book and read several pages. *Fellowship of the Ring* became a source of solace for Finnian, the words of Tolkien's characters offered wisdom and hope in the wilderness. He drew strength from lines which echoed in his mind whenever he felt the weight of his circumstances.

A particular line suddenly piqued his interest. *All we have to decide is what to do with the time that is given to us.* Gandalf's words probed his heart and mind like the wakeup call he so desperately needed. Like a flicker of lightning on a dark night, an idea sparked within him. Perhaps he was able to use parts from the wreckage to construct a distress beacon and finally have a chance of being rescued.

As he gathered what he needed, Finnian's emotions were in turmoil. Desperation fuelled his spirit to make something, anything, that might save him, as restlessness drove him to scavenge tirelessly.

But as the sun began to set and the cold air crept in, Finnian's body rebelled against the strenuous pursuit. His hands went numb from the cold and his wrist throbbed with pain. Still, he found himself unable to cease. The thought of giving up and accepting his fate was not an option. He was tired of waiting.

As he surveyed his modest assortment of salvaged parts, Finnian couldn't resist feeling conflicted. On one hand, he was exhausted and doubtful about his chances for success. On the other hand, a glimmer of desire and ambition sparked within him that had been absent for so long.

The upcoming days would be filled with challenges, but Finnian refused to give up. He would see this through until the end, even if it meant facing harsh weather and exhausting himself further. As he huddled inside the plane for the night, the wooden bear totem now hung from his neck from a piece of thin cable, provided some comfort and reassurance.

This project might in the end turn out to be futile, but Finnian found himself unable to resist feeling a deep sense optimism.

There is always hope.

BAREE

Baree drove through winding roads until she reached the secluded lookout. The engine's quiet hum ceased as she turned off the ignition, leaving behind a comfortable silence in its wake. Surrounded by dense forest, this spot offered the solitude that Baree craved. She had driven aimlessly for hours, with no destination in mind, just the desperate need to escape and clear her thoughts. As she stepped out of the car, her feet sinking into soft dirt, the scent of pine and earth enveloped her. The night sky above was a tapestry of stars, twinkling brilliantly against the inky blackness. Baree took a deep breath and climbed onto the hood of her car; the metal still warm from the drive. She leaned back, resting her head on the windshield, and let out a long sigh.

The vast expanse of stars above seemed to stretch on forever, offering a sense of peace within the chaos of her mind. Yet, even as she admired their beauty, Baree's thoughts inevitably wandered to Finnian. She wondered where he was, if he was safe, if he was even still alive. The uncertainty gnawed at her, but being surrounded by such natural beauty brought a small measure of comfort.

With eyes fixed on the starry sky above, Baree traced patterns among them with her gaze. Her imagination ran wild as she pictured Finnian somewhere out there, looking up at the same constellations. The connection, though distant, felt real and brought a sense of succour to her troubled heart. The stars became her silent confidants, holding her secrets and her hopes.

As the cool night air brushed against her skin, Baree pulled her knees to her chest and wrapped her arms around herself. It was as if she could physically hold on to the fragile aspiration that Finnian would one day be found. Lost in thought, she stayed perched on the hood of her car for hours, embraced by the peaceful stillness of the night. In that moment, she didn't have a clear path forward, but she found a sliver of peace amidst the unrest in her heart.

FINNIAN

Beneath the vast, star-speckled sky, Finnian lay on his back, eyes fixed on the endless expanse above. Each glistening light was a distant world, a reminder of the boundless beauty of the universe. The Milky Way stretched across the night like a luminous river, a cosmic symphony playing out in shades of soft blue and milky white.

In the peaceful stillness, Finnian felt a profound sense of connection to something greater than himself. For so long he had been confined, trapped in a city where artificial lights drowned out the celestial wonders above. And during his time in prison, the night sky had been stolen from him - two years of darkness.
Emptiness.

Emotions churned within him as he took in the magnificence above. Tears threatened to fall as he allowed himself to fully absorb this moment, this breathtaking spectacle that seemed like a gift from the universe itself. A silent tribute to the world's indescribable beauty that he was only now rediscovering. As twilight deepened and the sky darkened further, fireflies appeared, flickering like tiny stars brought down to earth. Finnian watched in awe as they danced around him, their gentle glow adding to the magic of the forest. One landed on his hand, its soft light casting a warm glow upon his skin.

In that moment, Finnian felt a spark of hope ignite within him - one that matched the firefly's gentle illumination. Underneath a sky full of stars and surrounded by nature's symphony, he found solace and connection with the world around him.

He stayed there for hours, lost in the vast expanse above and mesmerised by the dance of fireflies around him. The cool night air brushed against his skin, carrying with it a sense of cleansing and release from all that had haunted him before.

As the night wore on, Finnian allowed himself to drift into a peaceful sleep, cocooned by the gentle glow of the fireflies and the distant twinkle of stars. In the heart of the rainforest, he found a moment of respite - a brief intermission from the trials of survival.

With each passing dawn came new challenges, but in this moment, he simply existed in harmony with the world around him. The stars and fireflies had reminded him of the enduring beauty and wonder that surrounded him, even in the face of adversity. And with that realisation came a deepened obstinacy to keep moving forward, to find his way back home, and to cherish every fleeting yet profound moment of connection and peace along the way.

SEARCH AND RESCUE

The helicopter blades cut through the thick, damp air above the dense rainforest, creating a steady hum that reverberated through the trees. Inside the aircraft, the members of the search and rescue team were laser-focused, their eyes scanning the endless green below. A call from Sitka Airlines had given them a glimmer of faith - a plane lost in a storm, potentially linked to the missing man, Finnian Leif.

As they circled overhead, pilot Logan adjusted their course according to the coordinates provided. They had been scouring the forest for hours with little luck, but that changed when Logan's sharp eyes caught a flash of metal. "Look over there!" he yelled over the deafening noise of the engines, pointing to a spot where sunlight reflected off something shiny.

The team leaned in, straining to see through the thick foliage. It was faint, but unmistakable - a glint of silver in all the green.

"We're descending now," Logan declared.

The helicopter descended slowly, hovering just above the tree line. The vegetation was too dense to land, but they could get close enough to investigate further. As the rotor wash tore through the canopy, glimpses of what lay beneath were revealed.

"There it is," one of the team members announced while peering through binoculars. "Wreckage... definitely a plane. This must be it."

Excitement and urgency filled the cramped space inside the helicopter. They lowered a harness, preparing to rappel down and examine the wreckage. In this moment, every second counted, and every detail mattered as they worked towards solving the mystery of Finnian Leif's disappearance.

Hovering above this scene, they were acutely aware that the forest held its secrets tightly. But today, they were closer than ever before to uncovering them.

The helicopter maintained a steady hover above the wreckage, its team observing the twisted metal pieces scattered among the thick foliage below. Logan's voice echoed through their headsets, breaking the tense silence.

"Our tower detected a distress beacon a few days ago, but it disappeared before we could get any coordinates," he disclosed with a troubled expression. "Trudy, our ATC, thought she was going wild."

One of the team members turned to Logan with a mixture of curiosity and anxiety on their face. "So, we're certain this is Finnian Leif's aircraft?" Logan nodded; his gaze fixed on the forest below. "It's our strongest lead in months. That beacon could have been his attempt to signal for help before everything went silent again."

The trees swayed under the force of the helicopter's rotor blades as the team prepared to descend, and they all felt the weight of the situation. This wasn't just about finding wreckage; it was about unravelling the mystery behind Finnian's disappearance and determining if he was still alive, fighting for survival out there somewhere.

The deafening roar of the helicopter's propellers drowned out all other sounds as it hovered dangerously close to the dense canopy below. Logan's hands were tight on the controls, his eyes scanning the ground with intense focus. The team members crowded around him; their gaze fixed on the wreckage that lay buried beneath the thick foliage.

With expert precision, Logan maneuvered the aircraft, navigating through the tangled branches and twisted trunks to give them a closer look. And there it was, within the debris and destruction, a twinkle of hope in the form of a familiar tail wing.

"It's Finnian's plane!" one of the team members exclaimed, her voice trembling with emotion.

Logan felt a surge of adrenaline rush through his veins as he brought the helicopter even closer. As they circled around, the registration number on the tail wing came into sharp focus, N193E, confirming what they had all been desperately hoping for.

A wave of relief and exhilaration swept over the crew, their voices erupting into cheers that filled the cramped space of the helicopter. Months of relentless searching and uncertainty had finally led them to this moment.

But amidst the celebration, Logan's voice cut through like a beacon of purpose. "We still have work to do, team. Let's find a safe place to land and bring this man home."

The helicopter hovered precariously above the dense jungle canopy. They were on the edge of danger, so close to their target they could practically taste victory. The air was thick with tension, each member of the team bracing for what was to come.

Out of nowhere, a violent jolt shook the entire aircraft. Logan's heart jumped to his throat as he realised, they had struck a massive Sitka spruce tree, causing the helicopter to spiral out of control. The impact slammed the team members against their restraints, sending them careening towards one side of the cabin.

"Brace yourselves!" Logan yelled, his voice barely audible over the deafening roar of the engines and the screaming blades. He fought with all his might to regain control, but the helicopter continued its wild descent towards the unforgiving earth below.

The world outside became a blur of green and blue, the towering trees whizzing past in a sickening whirl. Panic consumed the cabin as everyone clung onto anything they could. The odds of survival seemed slim as Logan struggled to keep the helicopter from crashing into the unforgiving jungle.

Grinding his teeth, Logan battled with every ounce of strength he had left. But as the ground rushed up to meet them with terrifying speed, he knew that their chances of making it out alive were slim at best.

BAREE

Baree scrubbed the bar with ferocity, her mind racing with thoughts and emotions. The noise of the bustling bar faded away as she plunged into a deep reverie, only to be jerked back to reality when a customer frantically waved for her attention.

"Can you turn up the TV?" they demanded, their finger pointing urgently to the screen behind the bar. "Breaking news!"

Baree's hand shook as she reached for the remote, turning up the volume until the voice of the news anchor echoed through the room.

"We have breaking news from British Columbia," the anchor announced gravely. "The missing person, Finnian Leif's plane, has been found in a remote part of the Great Bear Rainforest after months of intensive searching." Baree's heart stopped, fear gripping her like icy hands. She leaned closer to the screen, unable to tear her eyes away.

"But tragedy has struck," the anchor continued. "The search and rescue team that located the wreckage has gone

190

down in a helicopter crash. No survivors have been reported at this time. More teams are being sent to the scene in a desperate attempt to find any survivors."

Tears streamed down Baree's face as she struggled to comprehend the devastating news. The room seemed to spin around her, everything fading away except for the urgent words coming from the television.

The anchor's voice grew more urgent. "The helicopter crash sparked a wildfire in the dense forest, making it impossible for any aircraft to reach the location. Ground crews must first extinguish the blaze before any rescue attempts can be made. Time is running out."

After being struck in the gut, Baree's knees gave way, experiencing a sensation akin to being punched. She clung to the edge of the bar for support, overwhelmed and helpless by the gravity of the situation. Finnian, along with those trying to save him, were now facing even more danger. She couldn't just stand by and do nothing.

Baree's hands trembled as she dialled the number for the Canadian Coast Guard. She knew this was a risky move, but Finnian's life was on the line, and she had to do something. The phone rang several times before a gruff voice answered.

"Canadian Coast Guard, Officer Thompson speaking. How can I assist you?"

Baree swallowed hard, trying to control the shaking in her voice. "Hi, Officer Thompson. This is Baree. My friend and I need information about accessing the Great Bear Rainforest by boat. We're determined to get in there, but we're not sure if our small vessel can handle it."

Officer Thompson let out an exasperated sigh. "Baree, do you understand the dangers of navigating the Great Bear Rainforest? It's one of the most remote and treacherous regions out there. Smaller boats like yours often don't make it past the rugged coastline and unpredictable waters."

Baree's heart sank. She couldn't believe what she was hearing. "So, you're saying it's impossible for us to go in with our boat?"

"That's right," replied Officer Thompson firmly. "Without proper equipment, experience, and support, you'd be risking your lives. The forest is dense, and the terrain is unforgiving. It would be like signing up for a suicide mission."

Baree clenched her fists, feeling both frustrated and desperate. "Is there any other way to get in? Maybe a guide or a larger vessel?"

Officer Thompson paused before answering. "Local tour operators who specialize in this area are available for you to contact. They have the skills and equipment needed to navigate safely. But even then, it's not a decision to be taken lightly. Do you know where in the rainforest you wish to go, it's pretty big ma'am."

"Thank you for your help," said Baree softly before hanging up the phone. She sat there for a moment, her mind racing. She was not capable of letting herself be dissuaded now. Finnian's life depended on her finding a way into that forest. But the more she thought about it, the more daunting the challenge seemed.

FINNIAN

Finnian found himself huddled inside the wreckage of his plane, where he relocated his makeshift shelter for improved protection from the elements just before winter had arrived. Weak and nauseous, he experienced discomfort after consuming tainted prey that caused illness once more. The cramped interior of the plane was suffocating; his body wracked with fever and chills as he drifted in and out of restless sleep.

Suddenly, a loud crash jolted him awake. The sound echoed through the forest, startling birds and animals alike. Finnian's heart raced in his chest as he struggled to sit up, the disorientation and sickness making it hard to comprehend what had just happened.

He peered through the broken windows of the plane, his mind racing. He noticed something crashed close by, and the urgency of the situation pierced through his fevered haze. The possibility of rescue flickered in his mind, but so did the fear of further danger.

Despite his weakened state, Finnian knew he had to investigate. He found himself with no option other than to seize every chance of being found, while also needing to be cautious. Every movement was a struggle, but the crash had reignited faith in his heart. He gathered what little strength remained and got ready to venture out into the dense forest once more.

Finnian stumbled out of the plane; his body immediately drenched in a scorching wave of heat. The once serene forest was now ablaze, alive with roaring flames and the acrid stench of smoke. In the distance, he saw the twisted metal skeleton of a helicopter, now nothing more than a burning wreck.

Through blurred vision and ringing ears, Finnian's gaze fell upon the towering Sitka spruce trees as they were devoured by the inferno. The crackling and snapping of burning wood drowned out all other sounds, filling him with a sense of dread as he realised how quickly the fire was spreading.

His heart raced as he remembered the bear that he had encountered earlier in this remote wilderness, fearing for its safety amidst the raging blaze. With every step, Finnian's lungs burned from the thick smoke and his legs threatened to give out from exhaustion. But he pushed on, driven by desperation to find shelter for both him and the bear.

Finnian shouted hoarsely, hoping that the bear, seeking refuge in the cave where he was last spotted, reached safety. His voice got drowned out by the roar of the fire, yet he persisted in calling out against all odds. Every passing second seemed like an eternity as panic surged through him, aware that their lives hung in the balance in this fiery hell.

IGRIT

Sitting in her living room, Igrit was enjoying a peaceful evening until the news abruptly shattered her calm. As she listened to the urgent tone of the anchor, her heart began to race, and dread crept up her spine.

The words struck like a blow, hitting home as she heard the registration number of the missing plane- November One-Niner-Three-Echo. It was Finnian's plane, the one that her son John had left him before his tragic accident. Memories flooded back with painful clarity, bringing forth a mix of emotions that overwhelmed Igrit.

"MARTY!" she yelled, her panicked voice rushing through the house, in a daze, she reached for her phone and dialled Grace's number, her trembling fingers struggling to press the buttons. When Grace answered, she struggled to find her voice, barely managing to convey the devastating news. "Turn on your television, Grace. They've found him," she uttered through tears.

As she hung up, Igrit felt lost and alone. The once welcoming living room now became a place of sorrow and regret. She stared at the television screen, listening to the report continue in the background as tears streamed down her face. Marty rushed into the living room and was by her side in an instant. He clutched her slumping body as her feet gave way. Together they sat on the floor, glaring at the television set.

Once again, she was forced to confront the loss of her son, with the loss of Finnian.

FINNIAN

The bear's nostrils flare, choking on the overwhelming scent of smoke that invades its den. Instincts, long dormant, ignite with a primal urgency. Its sanctuary is under threat; fire rages towards it, threatening to consume everything in its path. The human it has reluctantly accepted as a companion stirs, barely conscious from the suffocating fumes.

The bear growls low in its throat, nudging the human's leg with a sense of urgency. Finnian stumbles alongside the enormous beast, relying on it for support as they navigate through the thick smoke and chaos. With each laborious step, they dodge flames and debris, guided only by the bear's keen instincts.

Days blur together in a haze of ash and struggle. The bear leads the way, pausing only briefly for rest and water before pushing forward once more. Finnian is driven by sheer desire and the unwavering presence of his unlikely ally.

Upon emerging from the smouldering remains of the forest, they were met with a towering fence blocking their path.

The bear paces with a sense of unease, urgently barking commands at Finnian. They have come too far to be stopped now; there must be a way through.

Finnian examines every inch of the fence, searching for any weakness or gap that could serve as a means of escape. The bear watches attentively, using guttural growls to urge him on. Exhaustion threatens to overtake them both, but they push through, united in their will to survive.

The fence appeared impenetrable. The strong wire and metal structure extended metres into the earth, designed to keep out digging animals. The bear stood, taking deep breaths, and inspected the barrier. It groaned and barked at Finnian, the sounds desperate and commanding. The message was clear: Find a way through.

Finnian understood the urgency. With trembling hands and raw determination, he pulled out an old tin can opener with a sharp edge. He began to cut through the wire, the metal protesting under his efforts but giving way bit by bit. The bear watched intently, its low growls of encouragement cutting through the crackle of distant flames.

On the other side, he waits eagerly for the bear to follow. With a mighty roar, the bear pushes itself through the small opening, emerging triumphantly on the other side.

The forest beyond the fence is untouched by flames, a welcome respite from the inferno they have just escaped. The bear stands tall and proud, surveying their surroundings with keen eyes, as if it has been here before. Finnian collapses onto the ground with exhaustion, but relief washes over him in waves.

GRACE

Grace sat on the couch; her eyes glazed over with worry. Patrick paced back and forth in the living room; the anxiety evident in his every step. They had been living in a state of limbo for months, each day filled with an agonizing blend of hope and despair. The silence was broken by the sudden beep of a news alert on their television.

"Breaking News: Plane of Missing Man, Finnian Leif, Found Near Princess Royal Island in the Great Bear Rainforest," the screen blared.

Grace fumbled with the remote, turning up the volume. They both froze, their breath caught in their throats as the newsreader's voice filled the room.

"Authorities have located the wreckage of Finnian Leif's plane in a remote part of the Great Bear Rainforest of British Columbia. The treacherous terrain and dense forest have made travel and rescue efforts extremely challenging. Rescue teams are facing significant obstacles in their mission to reach the site. Finnian Leif had let off a beacon which was tracked to the rainforest."

Grace's eyes filled with tears, her hands trembling as she clutched the armrest. "Patrick, they've found him," she whispered, her voice wavering. "He set a beacon. Patrick, he's alive," Grace repeated, her voice gaining strength as the reality of it sunk in.

The newsreader continued, "The remote location and unpredictable weather conditions have made it difficult for rescue teams to navigate. Efforts are underway to reach the wreckage, but the dense forest and treacherous travel conditions pose significant challenges."

The promise that had been buried deep within their hearts now surged to the surface, bringing with it a torrent of emotions. The fear of losing him again, the joy of possibly seeing him, the anxiety of the unknown, all mingled together in a chaotic storm.

As the news segment ended, they sat in silence, their hearts pounding. They knew the road ahead would be filled with uncertainty, but for the first time in months, a whisper of hope shone through the darkness.

Patrick, his expression set with perseverance, flew out of his armchair, grabbing his coat in a swift motion. He barged past Grace, his movements fuelled by a singular purpose.

"Patrick, where are you going?" Grace called after him, her voice tinged with worry and confusion.

"I'm going to find my son before I lose him too," Patrick muttered, his eyes steely with resolve.

Without another word, he rushed out of the house, ambition driving him forward. His thoughts raced as he headed for the airport; the urgency of his mission clear in every step.

But fate had other plans.

FINNIAN

Finnian's legs were like lead, each step a monumental effort. The forest around him had become a hazy blur, indistinguishable from one moment to the next. Time seemed to lose all meaning as starvation and dehydration gnawed at him, sapping his strength and will.

"Are we lost?" he groaned, dragging his feet behind him.

The canopy above blocked out most of the sunlight, casting the forest floor in perpetual twilight. Finnian stumbled forward, his vision swimming, the edges of his consciousness fraying with every passing moment. The growl of his empty stomach and the dryness of his mouth were constant reminders of his dire situation.

He could barely remember the last time he had found water or food. Everything had merged into a continuous, unending struggle for survival. Each footfall sent jolts of pain through his body, but he kept moving, driven by some primal instinct to stay alive.

The forest seemed endless, a labyrinth of trees and undergrowth that offered no reprieve. Finnian's thoughts grew fragmented, his mind a tangle of memories and hallucinations. He saw flashes of his past, moments of joy, sorrow, and regret, blending with the harsh reality of his present.

In his delirium, he imagined figures moving in the shadows, heard whispers in the rustling leaves. But he pushed on. Somewhere, somehow, he would find salvation. Finnian's journey had become a test of his very essence, a relentless battle against the elements and his own failing body, and the torment of his unprocessed trauma.

As he staggered onward, the forest closed in around him, a silent witness to his struggle. Finnian was alone, lost in the vast wilderness, but he kept moving, step by agonizing step.

Suddenly, a hut emerged from the tangle of trees and undergrowth, its weathered structure a beacon in the wilderness. A sign hung crookedly above the door, the words "Pullman's Treaty" barely legible through the grime and decay.

"Not all those who wander are lost."

With a sense of familiarity, the bear's behaviour shifted. It moved with confidence, its body language relaxed and assertive. The bear's head was held high, and it sniffed the air with an alert yet calm demeanour, almost like it was reacquainting itself with old smells and landmarks.

The bear started to mark its territory by rubbing its body against trees and scratching at the bark. Finnian watched in confusion as it rolled around on the ground playfully and groomed itself. Behaviour he had never seen before.

Despite his exhaustion, Finnian believed that perhaps seeing the bear's transformation was an indication they were on the right path.

The hut stood silent and foreboding, an enigma in the middle of the vast forest. Finnian took a deep breath, steeling himself for whatever lay ahead. He moved forward, each step bringing him closer to the unknown.

PATRICK

The sun was setting in a glorious display of oranges and pinks, casting a warm, golden hue over the winding highway. Patrick's mind was consumed with thoughts of Finnian. Suddenly, a sharp pain shot through his head like a bolt of lightning, causing his vision to blur and his body to convulse. He desperately tried to steady the wheel, but his limbs refused to cooperate. The car veered off the road, crashing violently into a tall oak tree with a sickening thud.

Meanwhile, Grace received the call she had always dreaded. Her heart raced with fear as she rushed to the hospital, her mind filled with images of Patrick lying injured on the side of the road. When she arrived, she found him in a hospital bed, his face ghostly pale and his breathing laboured. She took his hand in hers, tears streaming down her face as she prayed for him.

The dimly lit hospital room was filled with the sound of machines beeping and the quiet whisper of Grace's voice.

She sat next to Patrick's bedside. His eyes slowly fluttered open, revealing a mixture of pain and love as he looked at her.

"Grace," he managed to whisper, his voice trembling.

Tears streamed down Grace's face as she tried to stay strong for her husband. "You're going to be okay, Patrick. We need you. Finnian needs you."

Patrick squeezed her hand weakly, his grip faltering. "I'm sorry, Grace," he said with all the strength he had left. "I never told you... how much I love you. How much you mean to me."

Her heart shattered at his words. "Don't say that, Patrick," she begged through sobs. She noticed it in his eyes - their time together was approaching its end.

"I can't take this, Grace," Patrick's sobs echo through the hospital room, the machines beeping wildly with each heave of his chest. "Finnian was everything to me. Why couldn't I just tell him that? And John... I miss him so damn much."

His broken cries shake the bed; his body wracked with pain and grief.

"I'm furious, Grace. It's not right. Why does life keep punishing my son?

All I ever wanted was for him to find happiness."

Tears stream down Grace's face, her breaths coming out ragged and harsh. "Promise me, Grace. Find him. Bring my baby boy back home. Please...my baby boy." he spoke with a finality that broke her heart even more.

With a trembling hand, Patrick clung to his oxygen mask, struggling to catch his breath. Grace tried to comfort him, but the machines flashed red, and the alarms blared, drowning out their words. A team of nurses rushed into the room, pushing Grace out into the hallway. As she turned away, she collapsed into Baree's embrace, having arrived at the perfect moment in time.

The weight of the loss crashed down on Grace like a tidal wave, drowning her in sorrow. She had lost her beloved husband, her rock, and the father of her child all at once. The pain was indescribable - a void that would never be filled again.

In the days after Patrick's passing, Grace was lost in a sea of grief and emptiness. She couldn't escape the memories that haunted every corner of their once-happy home. But then Baree arrived, seeking refuge from her own demons.

The two women found solace in each other.

GRACE

They held the funeral on a crisp autumn afternoon, the kind that carried a sharp bite in the air despite the sun's feeble attempts to warm the earth. The leaves had turned vibrant shades of red and gold, a stark contrast to the sombre mood that hung heavy in the air. Grace stood at the entrance of the small chapel, her heart heavy and her mind numb. Patrick's absence was a gaping wound, raw and aching, and the cold did little to numb the pain.

As she looked out at the gathered crowd, Grace could see their solemn faces mirrored her own grief. Her eyes stung with unshed tears as she tried to focus on the service. It was a blur of sorrowful hymns, comforting words from the pastor, and the soft rustle of tissues as people wiped away their tears. But no matter how hard she tried; Grace couldn't shake off her thoughts consumed by memories of Patrick.

As the service ended and people approached her, offering condolences and words of comfort, Grace struggled to respond. Each conversation seemed like a fresh cut to her already bleeding heart. She was polite, nodding and thanking them, yet deep down she was overwhelmed, suffocated by their concern and curiosity. She wanted to scream; to tell them she didn't know anything about Finnian's whereabouts or if he was even alive.

After inhaling deeply, Grace attempted to calm herself while confronting the multitude of worried expressions. Tears threatened to spill over as she muttered a few polite responses through trembling lips. "We're still searching... No news yet... Please keep him in your prayers."

Unable to bear it any longer, Grace excused herself and stepped outside into the crisp air. Resting against the chapel wall, she allowed herself to sink under the weight of her grief. The questions about Finnian echoed in her mind, a cruel reminder of the uncertainty that still haunted her.

With tears streaming down her cheeks, Grace closed her eyes and whispered a prayer for strength, for answers, for a miracle. The world around her seemed cold and inhuman, yet she held on to the hope that somewhere, somehow, Finnian was still alive, fighting to return to her.

As the wind rustled the leaves around her, Grace stood alone in her grief, overwhelmed by the pain of losing Patrick and the fear of losing Finnian too. The funeral had been a heartbreaking farewell, but the search for her son was far from over.

JOHN

John and Finnian's plan to escape the stress of their lives by hiking in the forest rapidly turned into a nightmare. As they delved deeper into the woods, John's body began to betray him, his chest constricting with a sharp pain that made it impossible to take a full breath. He stumbled and fell to his knees, gasping for air as Finnian rushed to his side.

"What's happening?" Finnian asked, panicked as he saw his friend struggling to stay upright.

After John could only shake his head with little strength before the darkness took hold of him. When he came to, he was surrounded by blinding hospital lights and the sterile smell of antiseptic. The doctors' grim expressions were all too clear as they explained that John had been diagnosed with AIDS. Finnian felt like he had been punched in the gut as he tried to make sense of it all. How could this have happened? They were young and healthy, weren't they? But there was no time for questions or denial. John's condition was dire, and he needed immediate treatment. Finnian watched as tubes were inserted into his friend's body and machines beeped with each laboured breath, feeling powerless to intervene.

The reality of their situation hit him like a ton of bricks - their carefree days were over, replaced with endless hospital visits and tough decisions. But through it all, Finnian refused to leave John's side.

He sat by John's bed, watching as his once strong and vibrant friend wasted away before his eyes. The disease raged through John's body like wildfire, leaving nothing but destruction in its wake.

"I can't lose you," Finnian whispered with a trembling voice, firmly gripping John's hand.

John smiled softly, his voice almost a hoarse whisper.

"I'm not going anywhere. You're stuck with me."

As much as Finnian wanted to believe those words, the fear and uncertainty burdened his heart.

Two weeks later, Finnian arrived at the hospital again, his heart pounding in his chest. The sterile smell of antiseptic and the hum of fluorescent lights filled the air as he made his way through the corridors. He had dreaded this visit, knowing it would be confronting to see John in such a fragile state since his last visit.

As he approached John's room, he hesitated, the weight of his emotions threatening to overwhelm him. He could see through the small window in the door, John lying pale and still in the hospital bed. By his side, Marty sat slumped over, his head in his hands, the anguish of the situation etched into every line of his body.

Finnian couldn't bring himself to enter the room. Instead, he turned and saw Igrit standing in the hallway, her face a mask of worry and exhaustion. She looked up as he approached, her eyes red from crying.

"Finnian," she said softly, her voice trembling. "Thank you for coming." He nodded, swallowing hard as he tried to find the right words. "He looks worse. Why is it so rapid?"

Igrit shook her head, tears welling up again. "It's not good. The infection is severe, and with his immune system so compromised… they're doing everything they can, but…"

Her voice trailed off, the unspoken fears hanging heavily in the air. Finnian reached out and took her hand, offering what little comfort he could.

"He's strong, Igrit," Finnian said, trying to reassure her as much as himself.

"He'll fight through this."

Igrit squeezed his hand, her grip tight with desperation. "I hope so. He's always been a fighter."

They stood in silence for a moment, the sounds of the hospital a distant murmur. Finnian's mind raced with memories of John, the times they had shared, the laughter and camaraderie that had defined their friendship. Seeing him like this, so vulnerable and broken, was almost too much to bear.

"I don't know what to do," Igrit whispered, her voice breaking. "I feel so helpless."

Finnian looked into her eyes, his own filled with spirit. "We stay strong. For John. He needs us now more than ever."

Igrit nodded, wiping away her tears.

SEARCH AND RESCUE

As the recovery team made their way through the dense underbrush of the rainforest, their sharp eyes scanned every inch of terrain for any sign of Logan's crash. The snow had melted, revealing a tapestry of fallen leaves, moss, and scattered branches on the forest floor below. As they ventured deeper into the wilderness, one team member signalled for the group to stop.

"Over there," he pointed. "Do you see it? It looks like parts of a plane."

The rest of the team cautiously and quickly approached, eager to discover any evidence of Logan's whereabouts. As they got closer, the wreckage of a twisted fuselage became visible, partially hidden by the undergrowth. It was clear that someone had reinforced the plane and turned it into shelter from the elements. Layers of branches, moss, and mud covered its exterior, forming a protective barrier against harsh weather conditions.

One of the team members knelt by the plane and surveyed its exterior. He noticed deep scratches etched onto the metal, some fresh and others old. He called out to his teammates with a pensive tone in his voice.

"Look at these marks. What do you think could have caused them? Maybe a bear or wolves?"

Another team member joined him in studying the scratches. "It could be both; this area is full of wildlife. Whoever was here had to face more than just nature's wrath."

Inside the plane, signs of Finnian's survival efforts were evident. Makeshift shelves held dried berries, roots, and strips of meat. The reinforced walls spoke volumes about Finnian's resourcefulness to survive.

As they continued searching, another team member discovered an emergency beacon near the entrance covered in a thin layer of frost. He picked it up and examined it closely.

"Here's the beacon," he said, turning it over in his hands. "It seems to be ineffective."

The others gathered around, examining the malfunctioning beacon. It was clear that the harsh conditions had taken a toll on its delicate electronics, rendering it useless.

Despite Finnian's efforts to signal for help, the beacon had failed.

The team leader let out a weary sigh as he looked over the wreckage once more. "Let's document everything and keep searching. If Finnian was here, we need to find him. This place shows us that he's a survivor. He could still be out there."

The team nodded in agreement; their objective evident on their faces. They knew the forest was vast and unforgiving, but seeing evidence of Finnian's resilience gave them confidence. As they continued their search, a sense of urgency weighed heavy in their hearts; every second counted in their mission to bring Finnian home.

The recovery team moved through the charred forest, their feet crunching on the ashen ground. The choking smell of smoke filled their lungs, stinging and bitter. Trees lay shattered and smouldering around them, the remnants of the helicopter crash scattered like broken bones.

Jackson, the team leader, surveyed the wreckage with a clenched jaw and a heavy heart. His gaze fell upon the twisted metal of the rotor blades, one of which was embedded in a mammoth Sitka spruce tree. He could almost hear the sickening screech of metal against wood as it sheared off, sending the helicopter spiralling out of control.

"This is where it all went wrong," Jackson growled, his voice thick with regret. "If that damn blade hadn't hit that tree, we would have found Finnian."

Sarah crouched beside the wreckage; her fingers traced the scorched earth with a trembling hand. Tears welled in her eyes as she thought of how close they had been. "We were so close," she whispered. "If only we had more time..."

A grave silence fell over the group, each member grappling with their own feelings of guilt. Marcus broke the silence; his voice laced with frustration. "We can't give up now. He could still be out there."

FINNIAN

Finnian wandered through the forest, his vision blurred and his mind foggy from exhaustion and dehydration. The once familiar surroundings now twisted and distorted, the trees looming like spectres in the dim light. Each step felt like a monumental effort, his body heavy and uncooperative.

As he stumbled forward, he suddenly saw a figure in the distance. It was Baree, her form moving gracefully through the underbrush. His heart leaped, possibility igniting within him. "Baree!" he called out, his voice cracking with desperation. She didn't respond, continuing to move away from him.

Finnian broke into a run, his legs trembling with the effort. "Baree, wait!" he shouted, but she only moved faster, slipping through the trees like a ghost. He pushed himself harder, but no matter how fast he ran, the distance between them never seemed to close.

Panting and gasping for breath, Finnian slowed to a stop. Baree's figure vanished into the forest, leaving him alone once more. He collapsed to his knees, tears streaming down his face. His mind was a whirlwind of confusion and despair, the line between reality and hallucination blurring.

Suddenly, he heard a voice behind him. "Finnian, why are you running?" He turned and saw his father standing there, his expression stern and unyielding. Patrick's presence was a shock, a jarring intrusion into the nightmare that was unfolding around him.

"Dad?" Finnian croaked, his voice trembling. "Why are you here?"

Patrick's eyes bore into him, filled with disappointment and frustration. "Why do you think I don't love you, Finnian? Why can't you see how much I care?"

Finnian's heart ached, the words cutting deep. "You never showed it," he whispered, his voice breaking. "You were always so distant."

Patrick's form wavered, the edges of his figure blurring. "I tried, Finnian. I tried to be there for you, but I didn't know how."

Finnian reached out, but his father's form dissipated like mist, leaving him alone once again. The forest closed in around him, the oppressive silence pressing down on him like a weight.

Then, he saw another figure. It was John, standing just a few feet away. Finnian's breath caught in his throat, dread washing over him. "John?" he whispered; his voice barely audible.

John smiled, a sad, knowing look in his eyes. "Finnian, it's okay. I'm here." Finnian's heart broke, the reality of the situation crashing down on him.

"No, you're not," he choked out. "You're gone. You're dead."

John's smile faded away as his body vanished just like Patrick.

Finnian stumbled through the dense underbrush; his thoughts consumed by a whirlwind of despair. The forest around him seemed to close in, the trees towering like silent sentinels, indifferent to his pain. The memories of John's passing weighed heavily on his heart, each step feeling like a march through the shadows of his grief.

He found himself in a small clearing, the sky above a canopy of dark clouds. The air was thick with the scent of pine and earth, a reminder of the vastness that surrounded him. Finnian's chest tightened, the weight of his emotions threatening to suffocate him. He dropped to his knees, his body trembling with the force of his anguish.

"John!" he screamed, his voice echoing through the forest, a raw cry of pain and anger. He pounded the ground with his fists, tears streaming down his face. "Why did you have to go? Why did you leave me?"

The forest remained silent, the trees offering no comfort. Finnian's rage boiled over, his cries turning into incoherent shouts. He yelled at the sky, at the indifferent expanse above him. "It's not fair! It's not fair!"

He tore at the ground, his fingers clawing at the dirt and leaves. The physical exertion was a futile attempt to release the torment that churned inside him. The loss of John, his best friend, his brother in all but blood, was a wound that refused to heal.

"Why?" he sobbed, his voice breaking. "Why did it have to be you?"

The world around him blurred, his vision clouded by tears. He felt like a caged animal, trapped in the wilderness with no way to escape the crushing weight of his grief. The trees around him seemed to mock his pain, their silent presence a reminder of his isolation.

Finnian's cries grew hoarse, his throat raw from the intensity of his outburst. He curled up on the forest floor, his body shaking with sobs. The memories of John flooded his mind, the laughter, the shared adventures, the brotherhood that had defined their bond. The loss was unbearable, a void that nothing could fill.

"I can't do this without you," Finnian whispered, his voice barely audible. "I can't do this without you."

The forest remained cold, offering no comfort. Finnian's despair deepened, the darkness within him threatening to consume him entirely. He had never felt so alone, so lost in the vast expanse of the wilderness.

Finnian stumbled through the dense forest, each step a struggle against the relentless weight of his grief and exhaustion. His body felt like lead, every muscle protesting as he pushed himself forward. The forest around him was a blur of green and brown, the once vibrant colours now muted by his fatigue and despair.

He hadn't eaten in days, and his water supply had long run dry. Each swallow felt like sandpaper against his parched throat. His stomach twisted in knots, the pangs of hunger a constant reminder of his dire situation. But the physical discomfort paled in comparison to the emotional torment that raged within him.

The loss of John weighed heavily on his heart, a burden that threatened to crush him with every passing moment. Finnian's mind was a whirlwind of memories and regrets, each one cutting deeper than the last. He could still see John's smile, hear his laughter, feel the warmth of his presence. But those memories only served to highlight the void that now consumed him.

Finnian looked up at the sky. Tears streamed down his face, mingling with the dirt and sweat that covered his skin.

"I'm sorry, John," he whispered, his voice barely audible. "I should have been there for you. I should have done more."

The wind rustled through the leaves, a gentle whisper that seemed to mock his pain. Finnian's vision blurred, the world around him fading into a haze of tears and sorrow. He felt utterly alone, adrift in a sea of melancholy with no lifeline in sight.

"I'm sorry, John."

As he lay there, weakened by hunger and dehydration, Finnian's thoughts turned to the people he had left behind. He thought of his family, his friends, and the life he had once known. The longing for connection, for comfort, gnawed at him, a relentless ache that refused to be silenced.

"It's not my apology, Finnian," came the soft sound of John's voice. Finnian lifted his head, his eyes widening in shock and confusion as he saw himself standing before him. A looming shadow that threatened to charge.

"What?" he sniffled, climbing to his feet, "I don't understand."

"It wasn't your fault," the figure spoke again, this time its voice was an echo of his own.

"It was my fault. I was drinking," Finnian spat, "I deserve this, you deserve this. All of it!"

"Forgive yourself, Finnian. Or you'll be lost forever."

The figure began to flicker, morphing from a man into a bear.

With a final cry of anguish, Finnian closed his eyes, the darkness swallowing him whole. In that moment, he felt the weight of his grief and exhaustion press down on him, threatening to pull him under.

He was lost in the wilderness, alone with his sorrow and the memories that haunted him. The path ahead was uncertain, and the journey back to himself seemed impossibly far.

BAREE

Baree stood nervously on the tarmac, her eyes scanning the wild landscape that stretched out before her. The roar of the helicopter blades whipped her hair around her face, and she took a deep breath to steady herself. She had hired Lloyd, a seasoned pilot with a reputation for knowing the lay of the land better than anyone. Today, they were embarking on a mission that was as promising as it was desperate; to find Finnian.

Lloyd helped her into the helicopter, securing her headset and checking her safety harness. "Ready?" he asked, his voice crackling over the intercom.

Baree nodded, her heart pounding in anticipation. "Ready."

The helicopter lifted off, and soon they were soaring above the dense canopy of the rainforest. Baree gazed out the window, taking in the breathtaking beauty of the landscape below. The endless sea of vibrant green stretched out as far as the eye could see, interrupted only by winding rivers and cascading waterfalls. It was a place of wild, untamed majesty, and despite her anxiety, she couldn't help but feel a sense of awe.

As they flew deeper into the rainforest, Baree marvelled at the sheer vastness of it all. Towering Sitka spruces and ancient cedars stood like guardians, their branches creating an intricate tapestry beneath her. The sunlight filtered through the leaves, casting a dappled glow over everything below. Now and then, glimpses of wildlife were occasionally visible - deer drinking from a stream, a bald eagle soaring high above.

Suddenly, the dense canopy gave way to reveal a fenced-off area down below. Lloyd pointed it out to Baree with interest.

"See that down there? That's Pullman's Treaty."

Baree leaned in closer to observe the small log hut nestled among the trees.

"What is it?" she asked.

"It's an old sanctuary for bears," Lloyd explained. "There's a 1200kilometre or more radial fence around it, designed to keep bears in and wolves out. It's been left to nature for years now."

While they continued to move forward, flying for what seemed like hours over the endless expanse of forest, Baree

232

found herself unable to shake off the sense of awe and wonder that filled her. The rainforest seemed to stretch on forever, an untamed expanse that both daunted and inspired her. And then, suddenly, her breath caught in her throat as she spotted something glinting through the trees below - a wrecked plane.

"Lloyd, look!" she exclaimed, pointing frantically.

Lloyd expertly maneuvered the helicopter for a closer look. "N193E.

That's it. That's the plane," he confirmed, his voice tinged with excitement. "We've found it."

A surge of hope flooded through Baree's veins at the sight of Finnian's plane. She knew that this was just one piece of the puzzle, but it was a crucial one. Finnian was out there somewhere, and she wouldn't stop until she brought him home.

The helicopter hovered above the wreckage, its blades creating a deafening roar as it circled the area. Baree's sharp eyes scanned the ground below. Her heart raced as she searched for any signs of Finnian.

In an instant, her gaze caught movement near the edge of the clearing, a pack of wolves, their sleek forms prowling through the underbrush surrounding the area of the wreckage.

She exclaimed, "Lloyd, look over there," pointing to the wolves. "A pack of them."

Lloyd's expression turned serious as he followed her gaze. "Damn, that's not good."

Baree's heart sank as she realised the danger they were in. The wolves were too close to the clearing, making it impossible for them to land. She knew they couldn't risk it, but the frustration of missing such a crucial opportunity gnawed at her.

Lloyd stated, shaking his head, "We'll need to locate another spot." Baree's shoulders slumped with disappointment as she watched the wolves continue to move through the clearing, a cruel reminder of the untamed wilderness surrounding them.

She mumbled quietly with a touch of sadness, almost impossible to hear over the helicopter's noise.

Lloyd placed a comforting hand on her shoulder. "We'll find another way, Baree. This isn't the end."

As they continued their search for a safe landing spot, Baree clung to that small glimmer of hope. The journey to find Finnian was far from over, and though this setback was disheartening, she was determined to keep going. Finnian was out there somewhere, and she wouldn't stop until she found him.

FINNIAN

Alone in his cramped apartment, Finnian felt surrounded by a heavy weight that pressed down on him from all sides. A dimness filled the room, matching the darkness of his thoughts and emotions. Papers scattered across the floor reflected the chaos that consumed his mind. Empty bottles lined the windowsill, a silent witness to the countless nights spent trying to numb the pain.

Finnian's bloodshot eyes revealed just how tired he truly was as he ran a shaky hand through his messy hair. He had once been full of ambition and dreams, but now they perceived like distant memories fading into the void of his past mistakes.

As the shrill ring of his phone pierced the silence, Finnian couldn't bring himself to answer. He knew it was his mother, calling to check up on him as she often did. He was unable to confront her worry or letdown. The missed call notification on his phone screamed at him; his inability to connect with those who cared about him.

Moving around the room to rid himself of the suffocating despair, Finnian's thoughts were consumed by images of the night of the accident. The screeching tires, shattering glass, and cries of pain played over and over in his head like a never-ending nightmare. He turned to alcohol to escape the images of the mother and her child clinging to their lives, drowning himself in its numbing embrace. His life had become a blur of intoxication and regret, sinking dangerously close to alcohol poisoning every night. The once bright spark in his eyes had dulled, replaced by an emptiness that seemed to consume him. He knew he was spiralling out of control, but he was unable to find the strength to bring himself back from the brink.

A swift look at a photo on his bookshelf caused Finnian's heart to clench at the sight of him and John as young boys. John had always been more than a friend; he was like a brother to Finnian. He now faced a looming prison sentence while John slipped further toward death.

The guilt and shame burdened Finnian's conscience, leaving him like a mere shell of his former self. The burden of his turmoil was a persistent presence, dragging him deeper into the darkness. Tears filled Finnian's eyes as he sank to the floor.

He whispered a broken apology, barely audible through his sobs. He longed for some semblance of redemption.

Finnian woke from his dream with a start, the oppressive darkness of the forest enveloping him like a heavy blanket. He sensed the presence of the bear beside him; its warm breath tickled his face as it nudged him awake. The bear had returned from its hunt, its massive form looming over Finnian protectively.

With a low grunt, the bear pawed at the earth impatiently, urging Finnian to follow. In the faint moonlight filtering through the dense trees, Finnian noticed the determined set of the bear's posture. It wanted him to trust its instincts, just as they had done to survive in the unforgiving wilderness.

Taking a deep breath, Finnian rose to his feet, his body sore and stiff from countless days spent trudging through the rainforest. He rubbed his eyes, trying to shake off the lingering images of his dreams. The forest was shrouded in an eerie silence, broken only by the rustle of leaves and distant cries of nocturnal creatures.

The bear led him forward, its powerful paws making soft crunching sounds against the forest floor. Finnian followed closely behind, relying on the sound of its movement to guide him through the dark maze of trees and underbrush. His senses were heightened.

As they journeyed deeper into the heart of the forest, Finnian couldn't help but wonder what lay ahead. But he trusted in their bond - a bond that had become his lifeline in this wild and unpredictable place.

Time seemed to lose all meaning as they walked, the endless expanse of trees and shadows blurring together. Finnian's heart raced with anticipation, each step bringing them closer to an unknown destination.

Finally, they emerged into a small clearing bathed in silvery moonlight. The bear paused, its head tilting as if listening for something beyond human comprehension. Finnian stood still; his gaze fixed on his companion.

With another low grunt, the bear's eyes met Finnian's with a sense of urgency. It had found something - a sign in this unrelenting darkness. An advanced resolution filled Finnian's heart, knowing that they were one step closer to finding their way out of this wilderness.

Together, they pressed on, the bond between man and bear leading them through the night. The journey was far from over, but Finnian held onto the optimism that they would find their way to safety and survival.

The first light of dawn crept over the horizon, casting a soft glow through the towering trees of the rainforest. Finnian trailed onward, following the bear's steady pace, his footsteps sinking into the damp earth with each step. The night had been long and lonely, filled with the haunting calls of unknown creatures and the rustling of unseen beasts. But now, as the sun began to rise, its golden rays seemed to chase away the shadows and instil faith in Finnian's heart.

As they walked deeper into the forest, the dense canopy grew thicker and more vibrant. The trees towered above them, their lush leaves filtering the sunlight into a mesmerizing pattern of dappled greens and browns. Birds fluttered overhead, their melodic songs joining together in a symphony that echoed through the trees and into Finnian's soul.

The air was cool and refreshing, carrying with it a hint of mist that clung to the mossy ground. The scent of dew-covered foliage enveloped Finnian, invigorating him with each breath he took. He sensed life and connection to the ancient wilderness, guided by the bear who walked beside him with steadfast obstinacy.

As they approached a small stream, Finnian couldn't help but marvel at its clear waters, shimmering like liquid crystal in the morning light. The bear stopped to drink; its solid form reflected in the tranquil surface. Finnian knelt beside the stream, cupping his hands to drink deeply from its cool depths. The water soothed his parched throat and revitalised his weary body.

Continuing on their journey, they were greeted by an explosion of life as the sun rose higher in the sky. Vibrant ferns unfurled their fronds, delicate flowers bloomed in a variety of colours, and wildlife scurried about their business amidst the greenery.

Despite the challenges they had faced, both he and the bear had found strength in each other and in the world around them. The rising sun was a beacon that illuminated their path through the darkness and into the light. With revived spirits and a deepened bond, they pressed on.

The crisp, earthy scent of damp moss filled the air as Finnian followed closely behind the large grey bear. His heart raced with curiosity as they ventured deeper into the forest. The bear's determined pace brought them to a clearing, where the remnants of an old log hut stood hidden among the foliage. Thick vines covered its weathered wooden walls, and the sagging roof gave it a melancholic aura.

Finnian cautiously approached the abandoned log hut, the bear remaining by his side as a reassuring presence. To his surprise, the front door was still intact and swung perfectly on its hinges. As he stepped inside, he was immediately cloaked in a musty scent of the past. Sunlight filtered through broken windows, casting dancing dust motes around the cluttered space.

Among scattered papers and old photographs that were strewn across the floor, one caught Finnian's eye. It showed a couple standing proudly in front of the very hut he was in, their arms cradling a young bear cub. The caption read: "Jerry and Eleanor Pullman, Bear Conservationists, 1978."

As Finnian delved further into the papers, he discovered that Jerry and Eleanor had dedicated their lives to protecting endangered bears in this part of the forest. They had started a conservation campaign, working tirelessly to create a safe haven for these majestic creatures. Realization dawned on him that the bear who had been guiding him must have been one of their rescues - a cub they had nurtured and released back into the wild. This abandoned hut held memories of two passionate individuals who had made a significant impact on this forest and its inhabitants.

Finnian turned to the bear, a newfound understanding in his eyes. "You were one of theirs, weren't you?" he whispered. The bear's calm demeaner and ease around Finnian now made sense. This creature had known kindness and care from humans before.

Finnian's heart swelled with a sense of awe and deep connection as he stood inside the old, forgotten hut. The Pullmans and their work commanded his utmost respect, and he felt immense gratitude for the bear who had become his protector. In this hidden corner of the forest, he found a link to the past and a restored sense of purpose for the future.

As he explored the log hut, Finnian found more clues to the past, a rusted tin can, a worn-out blanket, and a weathered journal, its pages yellowed with age. He opened the journal carefully, the brittle pages crackling under his touch. The entries were written in a neat, flowing script, detailing the daily lives of those who had once called this place home.

One entry caught Finnian's eye:

"June 12, 1990. We've decided to stay here for the summer, to continue our work with the bears. The forest is a sanctuary, a place where we can make a difference. Jerry and I have seen so much beauty here, and we hope to protect it for future generations. Today, we released another cub, a small but significant step in our mission."

Finnian's heart ached as he read the words, the dedication and passion of the Pullmans palpable in every line. He felt a deep connection to their mission, a sense of duty to honour their legacy.

That afternoon, the bear led him to another hidden part of the forest, a wide, open area that starkly contrasted with the dense woodland surrounding it. Finnian followed the bear's lead, his curiosity piqued. As they broke through the last of the trees, he saw it, a long, overgrown runway, barely visible under the encroaching vegetation. The air was heavy with a sense of history, the memories of what once was lingering in the air.

"This must have been their way in and out," Finnian murmured, his eyes tracing the faded lines of the abandoned runway. The bear stood beside him, its presence a silent affirmation.

As he walked the length of the runway, Finnian couldn't help but think about the Pullmans. He had learned that Jerry and Eleanor had been killed by poachers, a tragic end to their noble efforts. Their deaths had led to a significant change in the forest's fate, a ban on hunting within a 2000km radius, the area now known as Pullman's Treaty.

Finnian paused at the edge of the runway, looking up at the sky.

"Why didn't I see this from above?" he wondered aloud. The canopy of trees that surrounded the runway must have hidden it from view, a natural veil concealing the remnants of the Pullmans' work. And who was to know how long it had been since the runway had been used? As he looked to down the runway, through squinted eyes he thought he could make out the faint, distinctive shape of an aircraft. A plane. He shook his head as if clearing the mirage from his mind.

The bear nudged him gently, breaking his reverie. Finnian turned to look at his companion, a new understanding dawning within him. The bear had brought him here for a reason, showing him the legacy of the people who had once cared for it. It was a poignant reminder of the interconnectedness of life, the impact of kindness and the enduring nature of heritage.

As Finnian and the bear left the abandoned runway behind, the forest around them seemed to close in, its secrets and stories wrapping them in a protective embrace. The path they followed wound through dense underbrush and towering trees; the air filled with the scent of pine and earth.

They walked in companionable silence, the bond between them growing stronger with each step. The bear led the way with a quiet confidence, its instincts guiding them through the labyrinthine forest. Finnian followed; his senses attuned to the subtle cues of the wilderness.

The sun dipped lower in the sky, casting long shadows that danced among the trees. As dusk approached, the bear paused at the edge of a small clearing. Finnian looked around, taking in the scene, the remnants of an old campsite, a circle of stones that had once held a fire, and a makeshift shelter that had long since fallen into disrepair.

Finnian's curiosity was piqued. He could see that this place held memories, echoes of those who had come before.

He knelt by the firepit, the stones cold and damp beneath his fingers. The bear watched him, its dark eyes reflecting the fading light.

A photo slipped out of the diary he still clutched in his grip. On the back it read *Amy and Dala, 1986*. Finnian looked at the bear before him, noticing its grey fur. He cast his eye over the photo again. The bear named Amy displayed large dapples of light grey and white over her fur, where the cub named Dala had only one white patch of fur on her lower belly, the rest of its body a light grey. Finnian cast his eye on the bear beside him again. It was completely grey. The bear was one of the Pullman's rescues, but perhaps not the bear named Dala. He tucked the diary away and continued to look around the campsite.

As night fell, Finnian and the bear settled into the clearing, the stars beginning to twinkle above them. The forest around them seemed to hold its breath, a reverent silence that spoke of respect for the past and hope for the future. Finnian looked at the bear.

"We'll make it through this," he whispered, the words a promise to himself, to the bear, and to the memory of the

Pullmans. The bear's gentle nudge against his shoulder was all the affirmation he needed.

BAREE

Baree mechanically wiped down the counter, her mind distant and preoccupied. After hearing the all-too-familiar mistake of her name from a customer, a twinge of resentment crept in. "It's Baree, like Marie, with a B. Not Bear-ee," she repeated for what seemed like the thousandth time.

But as she poured his beer, her thoughts drifted to Finnian once again. The discovery of his abandoned plane had injected a new energy into their small town, fuelling wild theories and speculations about his fate. Baree struggled to shake off her own inner turmoil, despite everyone else being filled with excitement.

She found herself pondering whether Finnian was truly out there, surviving off the land like a contemporary Tarzan, while her regulars gathered around the TV, engrossed in shows about wilderness survival. A part of her wanted to believe it. But another part of her resented the newfound obsession with survival skills and wondered if anyone truly understood the harsh reality of being stranded in the wilderness.

And in the centre of all the excitement and distraction, Baree found it impossible to disregard the persistent pang in her gut. She knew Finnian better than anyone else in town, and something didn't add up. Was he really out there somewhere, or was there more to the story? Her conflicted emotions only grew as she continued to pour drinks and listen to the wild theories of her customers. Each day might be filled with speculation and adventure now, but deep down, Baree couldn't rid herself of the sense of unease that consumed her thoughts whenever she thought of Finnian's disappearance.

Baree begrudgingly watched as her patrons' faces lit up with excitement, their eyes glued to the television. Wilderness survival shows had taken over their usual sports broadcasts, the screen now a constant reminder of Finnian, the one who got away. As they marvelled at the rugged landscapes and survival experts demonstrating their skills, Baree felt a twinge of jealousy for his ability to navigate and thrive in the wild.

"Did you see that, Baree?" one regular called out, his finger pointing toward the screen where a man was fashioning a snare trap from a piece of wire.

"Think Finnian's making traps like that out there?"

"Maybe," Baree replied nonchalantly, hiding her true feelings. "But he always did have an advantage growing up around here. He probably knows a few tricks those TV guys don't."

Another patron, a middle-aged woman with a penchant for knitting, chimed in. "I read about a guy who survived for weeks on nothing but wild berries and rainwater. Do you think Finnian's doing that? Seems like something he'd know how to do."

Across the bar, a group huddled together, debating the best ways to start a fire without matches. "You need dry tinder," one insisted. "Pine needles or dried grass. Anything that catches a spark easy."

"Nah," another interjected, shaking his head. "It's all about technique. If you can't get the friction right, it doesn't matter what you use."

Baree moved from customer to customer, refilling drinks and half-heartedly listening to the ongoing debates. One older gentleman, a former scout leader, held court near the end of the bar, demonstrating how to tie various knots that might be employed for shelter or traps. His hands moved with practiced ease, the knots forming in a blur of motion.

"This one here," he said, holding up a finished knot, "that's a bowline. Strong and easy to untie even after it's been under a load. Finnian would know it, for sure."

Baree found herself struggling with conflicting emotions. On one hand, she was proud of Finnian for his survival skills and ability to thrive in the wild. But on the other hand, there was a constant pang of disappointment that he had chosen this life instead of staying with her. And as she served drinks and listened to their animated discussions about Finnian's well-being, a tinge of bitterness crept in towards him for adding a spark of adventure to their otherwise mundane lives while leaving her behind.

Baree was wiping down the bar, her mind occupied with thoughts of Finnian. She couldn't stop wondering if he was still out there somewhere, fighting to come back to her. That's when he walked in - tall, relaxed, and with a smile that lit up the dim room. She noticed him right away and tried to push away the fluttering sensation in her chest.

He took a seat at the bar and their eyes met. He gave her an easy smile that made her heart skip a beat. "Hey there," he said, his voice warm and inviting, "I'll have whatever local brew you recommend."

Baree nodded, pulling a pint of the house favourite. "Coming right up," she said, trying to keep her voice steady.

"Thanks," he said after taking a sip. "I'm new in town. Name's Tom."

"Baree," she replied with a small smile, tucking a strand of hair behind her ear.

As they fell into easy conversation, Baree found herself enjoying Tom's company more than she thought possible. He embodied qualities of kindness, humour, and attractiveness - all that she wanted in a potential partner. But every time she responded with laughter to one of his jokes or experienced a spark of attraction towards him, guilt gnawed at her heart.

Finnian. She had only met the man a few times, yet there was an undeniable connection between them. The notion of being happy with someone else felt like a betrayal to Baree, given the town's hopeful anticipation of his return.

Tom reached out and lightly touched her hand, bringing her back from her thoughts. "You okay?" he asked with concern etched on his face.

Baree forced a smile and nodded. "Yeah, just... long day."

He seemed to understand and didn't press further, but even as they continued to talk and laugh, Baree's heart grew heavy. She couldn't deny the spark that ignited within her with Tom, but she also couldn't ignore the complicated tangle of emotions that accompanied it.

For a brief moment, she wasn't thinking about Finnian, and whether he was alive. She was relaxed. She felt happy.

FINNIAN

Finnian sat on the worn wooden floor of the Pullman hut, the flickering light of a lantern casting long shadows across the walls. The hut, with its rustic charm and remnants of the Pullmans' life, had become a refuge for him. He rummaged through an old, dust-covered drawer and pulled out a rolled-up map, eager to find some clue about his location.

Unrolling the map, he spread it out on the floor, his fingers tracing the contours of the land. The map was detailed, showing the vast expanse of the rainforest, its winding rivers, and the rugged coastline.

"Great Bear Rainforest," he said beneath his breath.

His eyes scanned the familiar landmarks, searching for any reference to the Pullmans' territory.

His heart quickened as he found a marked area labelled "Pullman's Treaty." It was a significant distance from where he had crashed. Finnian's gaze shifted to another part of the map;

a large island labelled Princess Royal Island. He traced the lines, the realisation dawning on him, this was where he was.

The island was remote, surrounded by treacherous waters and dense forest. A mix of relief and apprehension washed over him. Being aware of his location marked progress, yet the difficulties of his isolation became even more evident. Princess Royal Island was vast and unforgiving.

Finnian took a deep breath, letting the information sink in. He had hiked approximately 375 kilometres to Pullman's Treaty, from his crash site. The distance was daunting, but at least he now had a sense of direction.

Finnian sat cross-legged on the ground, surrounded by the remnants of Eleanor Pullman's notebooks. The old, weathered pages were filled with meticulous notes on bear behaviour, forest ecology, and the rich cultural history of the region. Each entry provided a glimpse into Eleanor's dedication and passion for the wild.

As he flipped through the pages, a particular section caught his eye. It detailed the indigenous groups of the Great Bear Rainforest, their territories, and their way of life.

Finnian's fingers traced the careful handwriting, absorbing the information. One entry stood out, the Gitga'at First Nation. Eleanor extensively wrote about their deep connection to the land, sustainable practices, and community in Hartley Bay.

Finnian's heart quickened. If he could find the Gitga'at people, they might help him find his way out of the forest. But as he continued reading, he realised just how far north their territory was. The rugged coastline, the dense forest, and the treacherous waters made the journey nearly impossible for him, especially without proper equipment or knowledge of the land.

He sighed, optimism fading as quickly as it appeared. The Gitga'at community was too far away, the risks too great. Finnian understood he needed to concentrate on surviving in the immediate area, utilizing the knowledge and resources available to him.

He carefully closed the notebook, a sense of resignation settling over him. Eleanor's words were a testimony to the resilience and strength of the indigenous people, but they also highlighted the challenges of navigating this vast, untamed wilderness. Finnian folded the notebook and tucked it safely into his pack, a reminder of the wisdom and guidance Eleanor left behind.

Frustration bubbled up inside him, a knot of helplessness tightening in his chest. The isolation was getting to him, the constant uncertainty, the struggle to find food, the relentless cold. The promise of finding the Gitga'at people quickly became a fleeting beacon, and now that it was gone, the weight of his situation bore down on him even harder.

Finnian's eyes glimmered with unshed tears as he looked around the forest that became both his prison and his sanctuary. He was alone, relying on the remnants of a stranger's notes and his own wits to survive. The enormity of it all threatened to overwhelm him, but he couldn't afford to succumb to despair. Not now.

With a deep breath, Finnian stood up, casting one last glance at the notes before turning back to the campsite. He couldn't escape the sense of unease when he thought about bunking inside the cabin.

The journey through the Great Bear Rainforest was far from over, but he was determined to face it with the same resilience and strength that Eleanor admired in the Gitga'at people.

Clutching the notebook to his chest, he whispered a silent vow to Eleanor, to himself, and to the vast wilderness around him. "I won't give up," he promised. "I'll find a way."

As he made his way back to the campsite, the shadows lengthening with the setting sun, Finnian felt purpose. Despite the unforgiving nature of the forest, he had learned to adapt and survive. The knowledge Eleanor had left behind was a lifeline, and he would use it to navigate the challenges that lay ahead. His journey was far from over.

ELEANOR

Eleanor Pullman had always been a woman of passion and intellect. As a psychology professor, she had dedicated her life to understanding the complexities of the human mind. But everything changed when she met Jerry. Their connection was immediate and profound, and soon after, she traded the halls of academia for the untamed beauty of the remote forest. Together, they formed the bear sanctuary, a testament to their shared love for wildlife and their commitment to conservation.

Eleanor immersed herself in the study of ethology, focusing primarily on bears. She documented the intricate behaviours and social structures of these magnificent creatures through observation and research, filling her days with this task. It was a calling that fulfilled her in ways she had never imagined, blending her expertise in psychology with her newfound passion for wildlife.

One fateful day, something shattered the sanctuary's tranquillity. A poacher had killed a grey mother bear, leaving behind two orphaned female cubs. Eleanor's heart broke at the sight of the tiny, trembling cubs. Without hesitation, she adopted them into the sanctuary, naming them Amy and Dala, a nod to the amygdala, the part of the brain responsible for processing emotions.

As Eleanor nurtured the cubs, she quickly noticed that Amy was different. Patches of her fur were white, a rare pigment condition that made her stand out. This unique feature also made her a target for poachers, as her pelt was valuable. Eleanor was determined to protect Amy and Dala, to give them the safe and loving environment they deserved.

She studied them diligently, her observations meticulous and insightful. She noted how Amy's condition affected her interactions with other bears, and how Dala, always by her sister's side, seemed to be her constant protector. Eleanor's research expanded, shedding light on the emotional and social lives of bears, their intelligence, and their capacity for empathy and resilience.

The sanctuary thrived under Eleanor and Jerry's care. Their work attracted attention from conservationists and researchers alike, who marvelled at the depth of understanding Eleanor brought to her studies. But to Eleanor, it was never about recognition. Eleanor focused on the bears, on Amy and

Dala, and on honouring the memory of the mother bear who had been taken from them.

In the quiet moments, as she watched Amy and Dala play under the canopy of trees, Eleanor felt a profound sense of peace. She had found her true calling, blending her knowledge of psychology with the wild, unpredictable beauty of nature. Her legacy lived on in every bear she protected, every life she touched, and every insight she shared with the world.

Though Eleanor and Jerry were no longer there to care for the sanctuary, their spirit endured. The forest, the bears, and the Pullman's dedication to conservation became an enduring witness to their love and commitment. And in the heart of the wilderness, Amy and Dala thrived, carrying forward the legacy of the sanctuary's founders.

FINNIAN

Finnian settled near a shallow lake edge, the light of the day casting a warm glow over Eleanor Pullman's weathered notebook. He flipped through the pages, his eyes scanning the meticulous notes and drawings that documented her life's work. As he turned to a new section, he found himself drawn into the intriguing phenomenon Eleanor had recorded.

He read aloud to himself, finding comfort in the rhythm of his own voice. "The Kermode bear, also known as the Spirit bear, is a rare, white-furred black bear found on the northwest coast of British Columbia, particularly on Princess Royal Island. This unique coloration is due to a recessive gene at the melanocortin 1 receptor (MC1R) locus. For a bear to be born white, it must inherit this recessive gene from both parents."

Finnian paused, imagining the striking sight of a white bear moving through the dense forest. The idea seemed almost mystical; a natural marvel hidden within the wilderness.

He continued reading, "The white fur is a fascinating example of colour polymorphism in mammals. While black bears typically have dark fur, the presence of this recessive gene results in the rare white phase. Interestingly, some studies suggest that the white fur may provide a selective advantage during salmon hunting, as it allows the bears to blend in better with the snowy environment, or bright sunny sky."

The thought of these bears adapting to their surroundings, using their unique traits to survive, resonated with Finnian. He felt a kinship with the Spirit bear, both of them navigating the challenges of the wild, finding ways to endure. Finnian's eyes moved to the final paragraph, "The indigenous Kitasoo people have legends about these white bears, attributing their existence to supernatural forces. Science, however, explains it through genetics and natural selection."

He closed the notebook gently; the pages filled with Eleanor's insights and observations now etched into his mind. The story of the Spirit bear was more than just a tale of genetics; it embodied strength and adaptation, qualities he was coming to understand deeply in his own journey.

Finnian leaned back, the wooden bear in his pocket a comforting presence. As the night settled around him, he felt at ease. The forest held many secrets, and he was just beginning to uncover them, one discovery at a time.

He cast his eye toward the light grey bear he often referred to in mind as *Gandalf the grey.* The bear was frolicked near the shallow edge of the lake, playfully nudging and mouthing the otters that chattered and splashed around it. The sun shone down, casting sparkling golden rays upon the water's surface. With a graceful glide, the bear slipped into the water, the playful critters darting around it in a game of tag. The air was filled with the sounds of happy chatter and splashing water.

As the bear emerged from the water, Finnian noticed something curious. The half of the bear that had been submerged was significantly lighter than the other, its fur glistening with droplets of water. He climbed to his feet in wonder, having not noticed the change in her coat previous times she had gotten wet. He stepped cautiously toward the bear, drawn by both curiosity and a feeling of familiarity. The bear, oblivious to his approach, continued to play with the otters, their antics creating ripples in the lake.

Finnian's breath caught in his throat as the bear stood on its hind legs for a brief moment. In that instant, he caught sight of a distinctive white patch of fur on its lower belly. Curiosity flooded his mind as he reached into his pocket, pulling out a faded photograph of two young cubs. His eyes darted between the photo and the bear before him, comparing markings and features.

Overwhelmed with emotion, Finnian whispered aloud, "Dala."

At the sound of its name, the bear's front paws landed with a thud in the water, sending the otters scrambling for safety. It turned its head sharply, glaring in Finnian's direction. The moment seemed to stretch into eternity as they locked eyes. Slowly but surely, recognition dawned on the bear's face.

Without hesitation, it charged towards Finnian, who braced himself for an attack. But instead of aggression, the bear knocked him to the ground with its full weight, hovering its body over Finnian so as not to crush him. It covered his face with enthusiastic licks and nuzzles. It was unmistakable now. This bear, grown yet familiar, was indeed Dala - the cub that had been rescued alongside another, by the Pullmans. Overwhelmed with joy and disbelief, Finnian wrapped his arms around the bear in a tight embrace.

The bear's warm, wet tongue on his cheek brought him back to reality. This wasn't a dream. "Dala," he whispered again, his voice breaking with emotion,
"You're Dala."

And in that moment, it was as if they shared the same breath, the same heartbeat - a bond unbreakable by time or distance.

Finnian sat by the fire; the notebook open on his lap. He flipped through the pages, eager to absorb more of Eleanor Pullman's wisdom. The glow of the flames cast dancing shadows over the words, lending an almost mystical quality to the text. As he read, he came across a section that caught his attention, detailing the vital role of salmon carcasses in the forest ecosystem.

He began to read aloud, the rhythm of his voice merging with the crackle of the fire. "Salmon carcasses play a crucial role in nourishing the Great Bear Rainforest. When salmon die after spawning, animals often leave their bodies in and around the rivers. These nutrient-rich carcasses decompose and release important nutrients like nitrogen, phosphorus, and carbon into the soil. This process helps fertilize the trees and plants, promoting lush growth and a thriving ecosystem."

Finnian paused, imagining the salmon's journey from the ocean to the forest, their final act a gift to the land. He continued, "Bears, wolves, and other animals often drag the carcasses into the forest, spreading the nutrients even further from the rivers. As the nutrients from the salmon seep into the soil, they are taken up by the trees, leading to increased growth. The connection between salmon and the forest is so significant that researchers can study tree rings to understand past salmon runs."

He traced a finger along the page, marvelling at the intricate balance of nature Eleanor had captured in her notes. "When there are abundant salmon runs, more carcasses end up in the forest, leading to higher nutrient levels. This results in wider tree rings for those years, indicating a period of rapid growth. Conversely, years with poor salmon runs will show narrower tree rings, reflecting slower growth due to fewer nutrients."

The words resonated deeply with Finnian, the interconnectedness of the forest and its inhabitants mirroring his own struggle for survival. The cycle of life and death, of giving and receiving, was a powerful reminder of the resilience inherent in nature.

He closed the notebook gently, the firelight casting a warm glow over the pages. The story of the salmon's journey and its impact on the forest was more than just a tale of survival; it embodied the delicate harmony that sustained the Great Bear Rainforest.

As he stared into the flickering flames. He was part of this intricate web, and he had a role to play. The knowledge Eleanor had left behind was a lifeline, guiding him through the challenges of the wild. Each new finding strengthened his bond with the forest and the wisdom inherited from its ancient trees.

Finnian flipped through the pages again, his curiosity piqued by her detailed observations and unconventional methods. One entry caught his eye, its title intriguing: "Seed Dispersal through Bear Scat." He began to read aloud, fascinated by Eleanor's unique approach to forest regeneration.

"Bears play a crucial role in seed dispersal within the Great Bear Rainforest," Eleanor had written. "As they move through the forest, they consume a variety of fruits and berries. These seeds pass through their digestive system and are deposited in their scat, often far from the parent plant. This natural process helps to spread plant species and maintain the forest's biodiversity."

Finnian could almost hear Eleanor's voice as he continued, "To aid in reforestation efforts, I began collecting bear scat, which is rich in viable seeds. By redistributing these seeds, we can encourage growth in areas that are less dense in trees. Buckets of bear scat are particularly effective, as they contain a concentrated source of nutrients that promote healthy growth."

He chuckled at the thought of Eleanor lugging buckets of bear poop through the forest, her dedication to the ecosystem evident in every word. "I target areas that have experienced deforestation or natural disturbances," she had written. "The nutrient-rich bear scat provides an ideal environment for seedlings to take root and flourish. Over time, this method has proven successful in revitalizing the forest and supporting a diverse range of plant species."

Finnian marvelled at Eleanor's ingenuity and commitment to the land. Her understanding of the delicate balance within the ecosystem was profound, and her unconventional methods exhibited her deep connection to the forest. A sense of gratitude encased him for the knowledge she had shared, each page a treasure trove of insights and wisdom.

Closing the notebook, Finnian knew that every small action could have a significant impact on the environment. A familiar line from *Fellowship of the Ring* crossed his mind, echoed to his core. *All we have to decide is what to do with the time that is given to us.*

Inspired by Eleanor's example, he resolved to continue her efforts in his own way, contributing to the forest's growth and resilience. The legacy she had left behind was a guiding light, illuminating the path forward amidst the challenges of the wild.

Finnian moved through the dense underbrush with a primal grace, his senses on high alert. The forest surrounded him with a cacophony of rustling leaves and distant bird calls, but he remained attuned to every sound and movement. Survival in this wild environment required constant adaptation, a skill Finnian had mastered over the eighteen months he had spent alone.

With eyes like a hawk, Finnian scoured the ground for any sign of sustenance. It wasn't long before he stumbled upon a cluster of decaying logs at the base of an ancient oak. With skilled hands, he flipped one over to reveal a writhing mass of life: centipedes, beetles, and fat white grubs. He plucked the grubs without hesitation, each one struggling against his quick movements before being thrown into a pouch. These grubs were a vital source of protein, necessary to keep his strength up.

As he continued his journey through the forest, Finnian came upon a thicket that seemed perfect for setting snares. Skilfully using thin vines and sturdy twigs, he crafted traps designed to catch rabbits or small rodents. After placing them strategically and disguising them with leaves and debris, he set off once again in search of food.

He soon approached a low-hanging tree heavy with leaves and couldn't resist peeking inside a nearby bird's nest. His keen eye was rewarded with several small, speckled eggs, which he delicately removed from the nest - leaving the rest untouched for the mother bird.

As the sun began to sink lower in the sky, Finnian returned to check his snares. His heart pounded when he saw one had been triggered and cautiously approached it. His prize was a small rabbit, still struggling slightly. With swift precision and respect for its life, Finnian ended its struggle. The forest had once again provided for him.

Experiencing the gravity of his achievements, Finnian located a spot by a stream to ignite a fire. He ignited sparks into the tinder with flint and dried moss, then blew gently until flames erupted. The warmth and light were a welcome presence in the impinging darkness. He skinned the rabbit with ease and roasted it over the fire on a sharpened stick. The aroma of the cooking meat filled the air, tantalizing his senses.

Having sourced new tools, weapons and knowledge from the Pullman's cabin, his bounty increased, gratitude buzzing through every inch of his body.

As he waited for the rabbit to cook, Finnian cracked open one of the bird eggs and sipped its contents raw. It was rich and slightly bitter, but he savoured the nourishment it provided. Alongside the rabbit, he roasted the second egg and enjoyed the contrast of textures and flavours. For dessert, he indulged in a handful of roasted grubs, their crunchiness giving way to a surprisingly creamy centre.

By his fire, Finnian, while relishing his improvised meal, felt a profound tie to the land surrounding him. The forest was not just a place to survive anymore, but a teacher and provide offering lessons in resilience and gratitude. As he gazed into the flames, contemplating life and death and the cycle that sustained all living things, Finnian knew that each day in this wilderness was both a physical and spiritual journey of self-discovery and harmony with nature. As the stars began to twinkle above him, he lay back on soft moss, wrapped by the glow of the fire against the trees. In this wild world, Finnian found peace, strength, and an unbreakable bond with his surroundings.

He cast his mind back to a poem he came across in Eleanor's notebook beside a sketch of cubs Amy and Dala. He spoke each verse as he traversed through the rainforest on foot.

Beneath the ancient canopy, where sunlight softly breaks. A symphony of emerald hues, in every breath it takes.

The Great Bear Rainforest stands, a realm of mist and green. With rivers wild and mountains grand, an untouched, living dream.

Where Spirit bears in shadows roam, with fur as white as snow. And salmon leap through rushing streams, in nature's timeless flow.

The air is filled with whispered tales, of cedar, spruce, and pine. A tapestry of life and light, an endless, wild design.

In the depths, where shadows play, the echoes softly ring. Of wolves and eagles, in their way, their songs of freedom sing.

Here, the forest guards its heart, with secrets old and deep, a sanctuary for all life, in its embrace, we sleep.

In the quiet, hear the pulse, of earth and sky and sea, the Great Bear Rainforest calls, a song of wild, pure, free.

On slow and mundane days, he would often contemplate his endeavours with writing poetry and the remarkable artistry that can be achieved through words on a page. He found inspiration in the serene beauty of the rainforest every day, slowly learning to capture it in his own words within his mind or whispering gently beneath his breath as he worked.

BAREE

Baree stood in front of her mirror, smoothing out the delicate fabric of her dress. Despite the poised appearance of the reflection before her, inside, a tempest was brewing. Tonight was the night she would see Tom, a kind and attentive suitor who offered stability and security, unlike the untamed Finnian. She repeated to herself that this was the right choice.

Their date was pleasant enough, filled with laughter and polite conversation. But it lacked the spark that Baree had hoped for. Tom's laughter sounded hollow in her ears, and their words never seemed to truly touch her heart. As they exchanged goodbyes at her doorstep, with a chaste kiss on the cheek, Baree couldn't help but sense emptiness rather than fulfillment.

As she entered her empty home, the weight of her emotions finally caught up with her. The silence seemed to press down on her as she made her way through the house, each step echoing her solitude. When she reached the living room, the floodgates opened and all the feelings she had been pushing aside came crashing down on her like a tidal wave.

Tears streamed down her face, uncontrollable and unrelenting. She knew she owed nothing to Finnian, yet her heart seemed to believe otherwise. The evening with Tom only amplified what was missing, exposing the truth that Baree had been denying. She curled up on the couch, clutching a cushion as she let out gut-wrenching sobs that shook her entire body. In that moment, she realised that sometimes matters of the heart defy all logic and reason.

JERRY

Jerry Pullman had always been a guardian of the wild. From a young age, Jerry Pullman felt drawn to the vast, untamed landscapes that stretched beyond the horizon. His love for the wilderness was more than a passion; it was a calling that pulsed through his veins like the beating of drums. He dedicated every waking moment to protecting the forest and its inhabitants, particularly the bears that roamed free.

Years before Finnian's ordeal, Jerry had established the bear sanctuary, Pullman's Treaty, on Princess Royal Island. The sanctuary was his dream realised, a safe place where bears live free from human interference. He poured his heart and soul into the sanctuary, building it from the ground up with his own hands. Every fence and shelter, crafted with precision, stood as proof of his steadfast devotion, seamlessly integrating with the natural setting.

Jerry's partner in this endeavour was Eleanor, a kindred spirit who shared his love for the wild. Together, they built a life in the forest, their days filled with the sights and sounds of nature. They woke to the symphony of birdsong and fell asleep under a canopy of stars. Eleanor's tragic death at the hands of poachers shattered Jerry's world, leaving behind an emptiness that seemed impossible to fill.

But even in her absence, Eleanor remained a constant presence in Jerry's life. In moments when he was uncertain or beaten, he almost sensed her hand on his shoulder, guiding him forward. In the gentle rustle of leaves or the whisper of wind through branches, he heard her voice speaking words of encouragement.

Losing Eleanor also marked a turning point for Jerry. The sanctuary, once a place of peace and serenity, became a battleground as he launched a relentless campaign against the poachers. He knew every inch of the forest like the back of his hand and used his intricate knowledge to outsmart and drive out the intruders.

His traps and strategies were ingenious, turning the sanctuary into an impenetrable fortress that proved impossible for the poachers to breach.

Yet, the victory was bittersweet. With the poachers gone, Jerry found himself alone in the vast wilderness. Losing Eleanor was a wound that never fully healed, a constant reminder of the price he had paid to protect the sanctuary. But he refused to let her death be in vain and remained vigilant, ensuring that the sanctuary remained a haven for the bears.

As time passed, Jerry became a figure of legend among the locals. His wisdom and experience were invaluable, and he was often sought by conservationists and wildlife enthusiasts. He continued to live in the forest, a solitary figure guarding over the sanctuary he had built with Eleanor. And though the joy that once filled his days had faded, his love for the wild never wavered.

The sanctuary thrived under Jerry's watchful eye, a testament to his unwavering dedication and resilience. In his solitude, he found solace and healing in the forest, surrounded by echoes of lives lived with purpose and passion. And as he gazed upon two cream-coloured bears, Amy and Dala, wandering through the forest, he believed they were connected to Eleanor, a physical manifestation of her love for the wild.

Somewhere in the vast expanse of the forest, Jerry continued his vigil, protecting the sanctuary and its inhabitants with fierce determination. The vision of Eleanor and the bears served as a constant reminder that love, and dedication have the ability to surpass even the most challenging of hardships.

Jerry's story was one of resilience, hope, and an unbreakable bond with nature, a legacy that would endure for generations to come.

Jerry would continue to be a guardian of the wilderness as long as trees whispered secrets and wildlife flourished. A guardian of Pullman's Treaty sanctuary, a ray of hope in the wild, and a symbol of the enduring connection between humans and nature.

FINNIAN

Finnian crouched low behind the dense thicket; his eyes locked on the lumbering form of a massive grizzly bear. Its thick fur rippled with each powerful step as it made its way towards a towering tree marked by scratch marks and the unmistakable hum of bees. Finnian's heart pounded in his chest as he watched, mesmerised, as the bear climbed up the rough bark with ease.

The bear moved with surprising grace for its size, its movements fluid and steady as it approached a large branch where a beehive dangled in a delicate balance. Finnian was filled with a mix of fear and fascination upon hearing the angry buzzing of the bees within the hive, all due to the bear's audacity.

With one swift motion, the bear swatted at the hive, sending bees into a frenzied cloud. But it remained undeterred, taking another swipe until a chunk of honeycomb broke free. After observing in amazement, Finnian watched as the bear descended rapidly, moving back to a safe distance to savour its prize.

Inspired by the bear's successful raid, Finnian noticed his own desire for sweet honey and the energy it would provide grow stronger. He gingerly emerged from his hiding spot and approached the tree, ears straining to listen for any signs of danger.

Finnian encircled his arms around the rough bark and started to ascend, relying on the bear's claw marks for footholds. His muscles strained with effort and his hands grew raw against the abrasive surface, but his underlying force to survive drove him upward.

As he reached the branch where the hive hung, Finnian paused to catch his breath. The air was thick with the humming of agitated bees, their presence a looming threat. But he steeled himself and reached out, delicately tugging at the honeycomb.

A piece broke off, oozing golden liquid, and for a moment, Finnian was overcome with triumph. But his victory was short-lived as the disturbance triggered a defensive rage in the bees. They swarmed around him, stinging any exposed skin. Finnian yelped in pain, almost losing his grip on the branch.

After a sense of urgency consumed him, he quickly packed the honeycomb into his pouch and started descending the tree. The bees pursued persistently, their angry buzz filling Finnian's ears. After feeling the sharp sting, he ran while flailing his arms at the air near his head.

After some time, he made it to a nearby stream and jumped into the cold water, experiencing its surprisingly invigorating impact on his stung skin. He surfaced carefully after the noise of angry insects had subsided.

After a series of deep breaths and tending to several stings, Finnian retrieved the hard-earned honeycomb from his pouch. As he relished its sweetness, he found himself chuckling at the absurdity of the task. The wilderness had a way of humbling even the most determined.

Finnian knew that survival in the wild required learning from every experience, both painful and triumphant. And as he licked the last of the honey from his fingers, he made a mental note: next time, leave the beehive raids to the bears.

The forest was alive with a haunting stillness, each rustle of leaves and bird call seeming to hold an ominous weight. Finnian moved cautiously through the underbrush, every sense on high alert. The memory of his last encounter with the grizzly bear hung heavy in his mind, a mix of awe and fear that fuelled his careful steps. He had prayed their paths wouldn't cross again, but in the unforgiving wilderness, nothing was certain.

As he turned a bend in the path, his heart froze in his chest. There, only twenty paces away, stood the massive form of the grizzly bear. Its dark silhouette towered against the backdrop of towering trees; its eyes locked onto Finnian's with a fierce intensity. A surge of adrenaline coursed through his veins as he braced himself for what might come next. This time, the bear seemed different - more tense, more focused.

Finnian's breaths came in shallow bursts as he fought to control his racing heart. He knew he couldn't afford to show fear, but every primal instinct in him screamed to run. Taking another step forward, the bear emitted a low growl that sent shivers down Finnian's spine. It was a warning, and a challenge rolled into one.

"Why have you returned?" Finnian whispered to himself, barely audible over the pounding of his own heartbeat.

He forced himself to steady his breathing and think rationally. He needed a plan, something to defend himself with if it came to that. But as much as he tried to remain calm and resolute, every muscle in his body begged him to flee.

Another step forward from the bear, its eyes never leaving Finnian's. The tension between them was penetrating, thickening the air around them. Slowly, Finnian reached for a knife at his belt, grateful for Jerry Pullman's armoury. He drew the knife, not as a weapon, but as a means of defence if necessary. He refused to let down his guard; his gaze locked with the bear's.

In that moment, time seemed to stand still. Each second stretched into an eternity as the rest of the forest faded into the background, leaving only Finnian and the grizzly in an intense standoff. He could almost sense the intelligence in the bear's eyes, a depth of understanding that both fascinated and terrified him.

Just as Finnian thought he couldn't take another second of the tense silence, the bear suddenly rose onto its hind legs, towering over him. It was a display of raw power and dominance that left him breathless and shaking. His mind raced with thoughts of what might come next.

But instead of attacking, the bear let out a long, deep roar that echoed through the forest - a declaration of its presence and strength. And then, just as abruptly as it had risen, the grizzly dropped back to all fours, its eyes still locked onto Finnian's.

For a moment, neither moved. The world held its breath as they stood frozen in time, their fates intertwined in this electrifying encounter. And then, as if satisfied with their interaction, the bear slowly turned and disappeared into the depths of the forest.

Finnian remained rooted to the spot for what felt like hours, his heart pounding and his body trembling with adrenaline. As he exhaled a shaky breath and tried to calm himself, he knew that something within him had shifted. He had stood his ground against one of nature's fiercest creatures and emerged stronger for it. The wilderness was a place of challenges and tests, and he was learning to meet them with a newfound resilience.

Upon swinging open the creaky door of the small shed by Pullman's old log cabin, Finnian was met with a pleasant surprise as his eyes widened in delight at the unexpected ATV nestled in the corner. Despite its chipped paint, the vehicle seemed to be in good condition.

While examining the ATV's frame, Finnian noticed that the key was in the ignition and the fuel gauge displayed nearly full. "Looks like my lucky day," he muttered with a grin.

Finnian took a moment to familiarize himself with the controls of the ATV after bringing it out of the shed. After a brief glance at the map, he noticed distinct sections within the treaty and was fascinated by the old airplane landing strip shown on it. If he could reach that spot again, he might be able to determine if the plane he saw was actually there or just a product of his mind. If his vision did not deceive him, maybe he could find a way to leave and seek assistance.

Inhaling deeply, Finnian climbed onto the ATV and activated the engine, glad to hear a noticeable sound above the forest's rustling. He revved the engine and followed the overgrown path towards his destination. Despite the bumpy ride over roots and rocks, it was still a faster mode of transportation than walking.

While navigating the winding path, Finnian vigilantly scanned for possible threats amid the blur of green and brown hues.

Finnian finally arrived at a gate that signalled the boundary of a treaty section after what seemed like hours. After dismounting his ATV, he opened the 6-foot gate and made his way towards the old runway.

Finnian's heart raced as he approached an old plane glistening in the sunlight. His eyes hadn't lied to him. He surveyed the wreckage of the plane, his mind buzzing with possibilities. His background in automotive engineering giving him a slim chance at repairing the aircraft. The daunting task was fuelled by thoughts of home. Of Baree.

He examined its exterior before entering the cockpit and pausing to breathe in wonder. The dusty interior was surprisingly well-preserved, with functional instruments and switches that needed a good service. Finnian set to work checking the gas lines, engine, and controls.

With the sunset casting a golden glow over the runway, he stopped to admire the beauty surrounding him. Despite the challenges, Finnian felt a revived purpose as he was now one step closer to survival with his ATV and plane.

In the thick forest, Finnian maneuvered the treacherous track back to the log cabin, the ATV's roar drowning out his ragged gasps. The short-lived thrill of uncovering the wreckage was soon overshadowed by sheer terror as he detected movement approaching him from behind. With his heart pounding in his chest, he looked back and saw a group of wolves chasing him, their eyes shining like burning embers in the faint light.

The ATV shot forward with frightening speed as Finnian stomped on the accelerator, feeling a surge of adrenaline. The wolves were persistent, with their legs moving quickly to close the distance. Panic set in as Finnian realised he couldn't outrun them. The gate he had previously entered was in sight, but it was no longer possible to try opening it without allowing the wolves through into the treaty.

Desperation took control as Finnian made a split-second decision. He drove the ATV as close to the gate as possible before killing the motor and launching himself at the fence in one swift motion. Adrenaline fuelled his ascent up the cold wired fence, but just as he was about to reach safety, a sharp pain shot through his ankle. A wolf had lunged and sunk its teeth into his flesh with terrifying force.

Finnian screamed in agony, thrashing wildly until his other foot connected with the wolf's head and he was able to break free. He landed on the other side of the tall fence, scrambling away from the danger. His eyes fell upon a pack of nine snarling wolves on the other side, their leader howling into the air. The rest joined in, their ear-splitting howls echoing through the forest and sending chills down Finnian's spine.

ELEANOR - 1986

July 5,

It's been a tough few weeks. I've heard whispers of poachers making their way into the Great Bear Rainforest. The threat they pose to the bears, especially the Kermode cub, Amy, is unbearable. She's just started exploring beyond the safety of her den, and the thought of her facing those monsters chills me to the bone. Her white and grey dappled fur makes her a prime target, and I have to keep her safe.

Amy's eyes are filled with curiosity and wonder. She's always so playful, tumbling around the clearing without a care in the world. It breaks my heart to think that innocence could be shattered by the poachers. Every time I see her, I'm reminded of the fragility of life in the wild and the responsibilities we carry as guardians.

July 12,

Today I noticed unusual tracks near the sanctuary perimeter. Heavy boot prints, and they didn't belong to any of our team. It's too close for comfort. I followed the trail for a while but lost it near the river. Whoever it is, they know what they're doing. I have to be more vigilant. Amy deserves the chance to grow up in a safe environment, without the constant fear of being hunted.

I spent the afternoon setting up more cameras around the sanctuary. Each lens feels like an extra set of eyes watching over the bears. The forest is dense, and shadows play tricks on my mind, but I can't afford to let my guard down.

July 19,

Amy and Dala were playful this morning, tumbling and pouncing around the clearing. I couldn't help but smile watching them together, but my heart was heavy. I set up more cameras around the sanctuary today. I'm determined to catch any intruders before they get too close. Every rustle in the underbrush sets me on edge, my heart pounding with anxiety.

I've started keeping a detailed log of all the comings and goings in the area. Each entry adds to my growing paranoia, but it's necessary. The bears' lives depend on it. I've also contacted a few wildlife experts for advice. Their insights are invaluable, but it's clear that we're facing a formidable adversary.

July 25,

Today, I found a snare. It was hidden well, but Dala's curiosity almost led her right into it. I dismantled it with shaking hands, my mind racing with anger and fear. These poachers are ruthless. It's clear they've breached our sanctuary. I've alerted the authorities, but out here, we're on our own. I must protect these bears with everything I have.

The sight of that snare was a gut punch. It's not just a threat; it's a violation of our sanctuary's sanctity. I've started carrying a small toolkit with me everywhere, ready to dismantle any traps I find. Every step in the forest feels fraught with danger now, but I refuse to let fear paralyse me.

August 1,

Last night was restless. I heard noises outside the cabin, but by the time I got out there, whoever it was had vanished into the night. It's getting too dangerous. Amy and Dala stayed close today, sensing my unease. I've reinforced the boundaries and double-checked every single trap I've set up. The poachers are getting bold, but so am I.

I've started leaving signs around the perimeter, warnings to any would-be intruders. They need to know that we're not an easy target. My nights are sleepless, filled with the sounds of the forest and my own racing thoughts. Every shadow holds a potential threat, but I'll do whatever it takes to protect my bears.

August 7,

I stumbled upon a campfire remains deep in the forest. They're getting closer. The poachers leave little trace, but enough for me to know they're watching, waiting for the perfect moment. It's hard not to feel powerless, but seeing the kermode cub twins gives me strength. Their playful antics remind me why I'm here and why I must keep fighting. Tonight, I'll set up extra traps and keep the radio close. We can't afford to let our guard down, not even for a moment.

August 10,

The tension is almost penetrating. Every noise, every rustle sends my heart racing. I've doubled the patrols and enlisted help from local volunteers, but the unease remains. Dala ventured farther from the den today, exploring the edges of the sanctuary. She's so fearless, so unaware of the dangers lurking just beyond the trees. Amy didn't move from my side. I spent hours watching, my heart in my throat, ready to intervene at the slightest sign of danger.

September 2,

The nights are getting cooler, and the days shorter. The shift in seasons brings with it a new set of challenges. The poachers haven't made a move in the past week, but the silence is unnerving. I know they're out there, waiting for the right moment. Amy and Dala's fur is starting to thicken in preparation for winter. She's growing so fast, and her spirit remains unbroken. I must ensure she sees another spring.

September 10,

Today was a small victory. We found and dismantled another set of traps. The poachers' persistence is disheartening, but every trap we dismantle is a step towards safeguarding the sanctuary. Amy watched from a distance; her curiosity piqued. It's as if she understands the danger in her own way. Dala's behaviour was odd today. She pawed at the earth and rolled amongst the leaves.

September 18,

I received a shipment of supplies today from a conservation group up north. Extra cameras, more robust traps, and some winter gear. It's comforting to know we're not alone in this fight. Amy seems to sense the changes. She's more cautious, sticking closer to the den. Dala's behaviour is increasingly concerning. I spent the afternoon reinforcing the perimeter and checking the cameras. The footage reveals nothing unusual, but I can't shake the feeling that something is coming.

September 25,

The forest was unusually quiet today. Even the birds seemed to hold their breath. Amy stayed by my side, Dala didn't. Our eyes watching every shadow. We spent the day patrolling the sanctuary, looking for signs of intrusion. As the sun set, I felt a sense of unease settle in.

October 1,

The first frost of the season covered the ground this morning. Winter is approaching. Amy's coat is thick and glossy. Dala has spent most of her days rolling in dirt patches and pawing the earth. Something is wrong.

We've had a quiet week, no signs of poachers. It's almost too quiet. I find myself jumping at every sound, every rustle of leaves. The stillness feels like the calm before the storm.

October 8,

Amy had a close call today. We were exploring the eastern edge of the sanctuary when she stumbled upon a snare. My heart stopped as she sniffed at it, unaware of the danger. I managed to call her away just in time. I dismantled the trap with shaking hands, anger boiling within me.

October 15,

The support has been overwhelming. It's heartening to see so many people come together to protect the sanctuary. Amy and Dala have become a symbol of our fight, their spirits embodying the resilience we all strive for.

October 22,

The first snowfall dusted the ground today, transforming the forest into a winter wonderland. Amy was cautious at first, but soon she was bounding through the snow. It was a moment of pure joy, a reminder of the beauty we're fighting to protect.

The poachers are still out there, but today, we won a small victory. Amy is safe, and for now, that's enough.

October 30,

I've been reflecting on the past few months. The constant vigilance, the fear, the small victories. It's been exhausting, but seeing Amy and Dala thrive makes it all worthwhile. The poachers have not made a significant move recently, but I know they're still a threat. Winter is here, and with it, a new set of challenges.

Though the snow makes it easier to watch for movement on the ground.

Eleanor's journal captures the ebb and flow of her emotions as she battles to protect Amy and Dala, and the sanctuary. Each entry reveals her unwavering passion and the small moments of joy and triumph that keep her going. Despite the constant threat of poachers, Eleanor's resolve remains unbroken, her love for the bears driving her to face each new challenge head-on.

FINNIAN

Finnian waited in anxious anticipation, bracing himself for the next leg of his journey. The encounter with the wolves had left him shaken and on high alert, his senses heightened for any potential danger. After days of rest and preparation, he set out to explore the log cabin, determined to find anything that could aid in his survival.

As he combed through each room, Finnian's heart raced with adrenaline at every creak and rustle in the surrounding forest. Shifting a false wall, he unexpectedly found Jerry's hidden armoury. His eyes widened as he took in the array of weapons and supplies, but his focus was drawn to a gleaming rifle mounted on the wall. He checked it carefully before slinging it over his shoulder. A newfound sense of security against the unknown threats lurking in the wilderness.

With grit fuelling him, Finnian made his way to the old runway. Each step felt heavier now that he knew the dangers lurking in the shadows. But he refused to let fear hold him back as he ventured into the quiet forest, inching closer to his goal.

As he reached the runway, he spotted movement on the far side. A massive bear emerged from the underbrush; its powerful form silhouetted against the morning light. It moved with purpose and confidence, a true survivor in its natural habitat. For a moment, Finnian felt a sense of camaraderie with this majestic creature.

The bear approached the plane with curiosity, observing Finnian as he worked on repairing it. Hours passed as he meticulously inspected every part of the aircraft, all while being watched by his wild companion. The sun rose higher in the sky, casting light over their makeshift repair site.

Finally, after what seemed like an eternity of tinkering and fine-tuning, Finnian climbed into the cockpit. With bated breath, he flicked switches and turned dials, his fingers moving with practiced expertise. The engine sputtered and roared before finally coming to life. A surge of relief and excitement rushed through Finnian as the plane rumbled down the runway, vibrations coursing through his body. He was grateful that he had cleared the path beforehand, knowing it would have been impossible otherwise. With a determined glint in his eye, Finnian took flight into the vastness of the unknown, ready to face whatever challenges lay ahead.

As the plane surged forward, Finnian's heart raced with a mix of adrenaline and fear. The wilderness had been his prison, but now he was flying above it, soaring towards freedom. His gaze flickered to the bear below, its eyes gleaming confusion as it ran alongside the plane.

But just as he allowed himself to believe in his escape, fate cruelly intervened. The engine sputtered and died, sending the aircraft plummeting back to the unforgiving earth. The impact rattled Finnian's bones, his mind reeling from the sudden change in fortune.

He emerged from the wreckage and was greeted by a chaotic scene. Smoke billowed from the burning plane, flames threatening to consume everything in their path. Anguish washed over him like a tidal wave as he realised that his chances of survival were dwindling by the second.

Finnian's composure shattered, giving way to rage and despair. He bellowed at the sky, cursing his misfortune and screaming for anyone or anything to hear him. But there was no answer except for the bear, watching with unblinking eyes from a safe distance.

The fire raged on, a mocking symbol of Finnian's failure. But he refused to give up. With every last ounce of strength, he dragged himself away from the inferno and into the safety of the forest. The bear followed close behind like a silent guardian.

Frantic thoughts raced through Finnian's mind as he stumbled through the darkness. He was still stranded in this godforsaken wilderness, still at the mercy of its brutal landscape. But he was alive, and that fact alone gave him a surge of obstinacy.

He would keep fighting, keep pushing through until he found his way back home. And if the bear chose to accompany him on this journey, then so be it.

Together, they would overcome any obstacle in their path.

So, as the flames died down behind them and the forest swallowed them whole once again, Finnian took a deep breath and kept moving forward. He was alive, and that was all that mattered.

Finnian made his way back to the log cabin, his mind a whirlwind of frustration. The wrecked plane had been a devastating blow, but he refused to give up. He rummaged through the cabin, searching for anything that might help him fix the plane once more. Supplies were scattered everywhere.

As he sifted through the clutter, his eyes landed on a dusty old beacon tucked away in a corner. His heart leaped with hopefulness. Carefully, he examined it, noting the wires and connections that needed repair. He spent the next hour meticulously fixing the beacon, his hands moving with a precision born from necessity. Each wire reconnected felt like a step closer to salvation.

Once the beacon was repaired, Finnian placed it in a prime position outside the cabin. He held his breath as he switched it on, watching with bated breath as the red light began to flash. Relief washed over him, and he allowed himself a moment to catch his breath. "Please, let this work," he whispered, his eyes locked on the blinking light. He knew he had to stay vigilant.

As he began to clean up his mess, a stack of papers on the desk caught his attention. They toppled to the floor, scattering across the worn wooden planks. Among the papers, an envelope stood out, its edges yellowed with age. Finnian's eyes widened as he recognized the signature: Jerry Pullman. With trembling hands, he opened the envelope, revealing a letter inside. The handwriting was neat but hurried, the ink smudged in places.

The poachers took everything from me. The sanctuary is lost. If you're finding this, they've taken me too, just as they did my sweet Eleanor. I buried her at the waterfall near the mouth of the river that runs to the sea. I hope her spirit finds its way out. - Jerry

Finnian's heart sank as he read the words, the weight of Jerry's despair pressing down on him. The sanctuary had been more than just a refuge for the bears; it had been a lifeline for Jerry and Eleanor. The loss and grief echoed through the letter, a haunting reminder of the cruelty of the poachers.

Determined, Finnian folded the letter and placed it carefully back in the envelope. His hands rummaged through the old desk once again, his eyes darting back and forth as he searched for any sign of escape. His fingers finally landed on a picture frame buried beneath a pile of yellowed documents. With trembling hands, he lifted it up and blew off the thick layer of dust to reveal an image that sparked a desperate hope within him.

It was Jerry, standing proudly beside a wooden canoe. The craftsmanship was evident; the canoe looking sturdy and well-made, as though it had been crafted with care and expertise against all odds. Driven by faith, Finnian made his way to the shed. With every step guided by the memory of the photograph, he pushed aside tools and supplies until his search led him to his salvation.

Hanging upside down from the rafters was the wooden canoe, just as the photograph had shown. Finnian's heart leaped with relief and purpose. He carefully lowered it to the ground, inspecting every inch for any signs of damage.

To his satisfaction, Jerry's craftsmanship had stood the test of time.

Finnian reached into his pocket and unfolded the map he had found earlier. *The waterfall at the mouth of the river*, it could be a clue, a direction to follow.

His eyes traced the lines of the river that snaked through the forest, leading all the way to safety. It would be a long journey fraught with danger, but it was his only chance at freedom.

He spent hours gathering supplies and packing them carefully into the canoe. Every item holding immense value in this treacherous landscape. The beacon's red light continued to flash, a beacon of hope in the vast wilderness.

JERRY

Jerry Pullman was a man of the forest, his rugged frame and weathered face from a life spent in constant battle against those who sought to harm the land he loved. Every tree, every stream, every hidden path was etched into his memory, like a map ingrained in his mind. Pullman's Treaty was a legacy, a refuge for the creatures that roamed free and wild.

But when poachers encroached on the sanctuary, Jerry's grief over Eleanor's death turned into unrelenting fury. He became one with the forest, his senses sharpened as he tracked the intruders like a predatory beast. His movements were swift and deadly as he navigated through the trees, his presence undetected.

The first camp of poachers was deep within the heart of the forest, concealed beneath a thick cover of ancient cedars. Jerry watched from a distance, his heart pounding with anger. These men had no respect for the land or its inhabitants, and Jerry would not stand for it.

With the skill and precision of a seasoned warrior, Jerry sabotaged their traps and snares without leaving a trace of his presence. It was a warning, a statement that this forest had a protector who would not allow it to be desecrated. But the poachers persisted, even as Jerry outsmarted them at every turn. He used his vast knowledge of the land to set cunningly disguised traps that turned the wilderness into an ally. Frustration brewed among the poachers as their plans continued to fail.

One night, under the cover of darkness, Jerry made his move. With his rifle at the ready, he approached their campfire with ferocity in his eyes. The poachers were caught off guard by his sudden appearance, frozen in shock at seeing this towering figure emerge from the shadows.

"This is my forest," Jerry's voice boomed across the clearing, commanding attention and respect. "You have no right to be here."

The poachers reached for their weapons in desperation, but Jerry was quicker. He fired a warning shot into the air, the sound reverberating through the trees. "Leave now, and don't come back," he declared with unwavering resolve. "The next shot won't miss."

Despite knowing the sanctuary would never be completely secure, he made it clear that he would protect it at all costs. The location of any poacher who entered the rainforest remained uncertain. Disappearances remained unquestioned.

With the treaty declared, the sanctuary flourished and thrived once again. Bears roamed without restraint as the forest gradually recovered from its old injuries.

Despite the passing of many years, Jerry was still considered a legend. His tale exemplified courage and loyalty, demonstrating the strong connection between humans and the natural world. He continued to live in harmony with the forest, a watchful eye always scanning for potential threats. Jerry remained alert in the vast expanse of trees and wilderness, fulfilling his roles as protector, caretaker, and guardian of the wild sanctuary he shared with Eleanor.

SEARCH AND RESCUE

Trudy's eyes were glued to the radar screen, her heart pounding in her chest as she detected the urgent beeping signal. The beacon's light flashed desperately, a desperate cry for help in the vast wilderness. Without a second to spare, she grabbed the radio and frantically called the rescue team. "We've got a signal!" she shouted, desperation lacing her voice. "It's coming from Pullman's Treaty, the abandoned bear sanctuary on Princess Royal Island."

The team moved with lightning-fast speed, their movements precise and efficient. The helicopter lifted off the ground, slicing through the thick morning fog as it raced towards the dense rainforest. As they neared their destination, the forest below grew thicker and more forbidding, its canopy forming an impenetrable barrier.

"We're getting closer," the pilot called out over the deafening sound of the rotors. "But there's nowhere to land. The forest is too dense."

Sarah and Dominic exchanged determined glances; their resolve stronger than ever. The helicopter hovered above the treetops as the airdrop hatch opened. With expert skill, Sarah and Dominic were lowered to the ground, their boots hitting the forest floor with a determined thud.

The helicopter remained in a holding pattern above, its powerful rotors churning as the ground team made their way towards their goal - an elusive cabin hidden deep within the dense jungle. The only sounds were those of their hurried footsteps and the distant hum of the helicopter. They navigated through brush and trees with ease, their training guiding them every step of the way.

As they approached the cabin, the beacon's red light shone brightly against the dark backdrop of trees. Sarah's heart raced with anticipation as she pushed open the door. Inside, they found nothing but an empty room. Dominic reached for a small piece of paper on the desk, his hands trembling slightly. He unfolded it carefully, revealing a hastily written message that spoke volumes about the desperation of its author.

The poachers took everything from me. The sanctuary is lost. If you're finding this, they've taken me too, just as they did my sweet Eleanor. I buried her at the waterfall near the mouth of the river that runs to the sea. I hope her spirit finds its way out. - Jerry

Sarah's breath caught in her throat as she read the note over Dominic's shoulder. It was a chilling reminder of the danger that still lurked in the forest and a haunting question lingered in her mind: where was Finnian? Had he found the note? Was he following the same path?

Dominic turned to her with a grave expression, his voice low and urgent. "We must find him. If he has followed this beacon, there's a chance he's headed towards that waterfall." Sarah nodded. "Let's move quickly. The helicopter will remain on standby. We need to reach that river and follow it to the sea.'

BAREE

Baree's hands moved frantically behind the bar, almost in a blur as she poured drink after drink for the rowdy patrons. The blaring TV above played a daytime football game, adding to the chaotic atmosphere. But Baree was used to it, the familiar noise and routine providing a sense of comfort and normalcy.

Suddenly, the screen flickered, and a breaking news alert cut through the game. Baree froze, her heart pounding as she watched the urgent report unfold. There was a possibility of finding Finnian Leif, who had been missing since his plane crash almost 2 years ago. a beacon had been traced at an old bear sanctuary 375 kilometres away from the crash site.

The bar fell silent as everyone's attention turned to the TV. Baree's grip on the beer tap loosened as she listened intently, emotions swirling within her like a storm. Relief washed over her at the possibility of Finnian being alive, but anxiety and fear lurked beneath the surface. Without hesitation, she reached for her phone and dialled a familiar number, her voice urgent and determined as she spoke with Lloyd. The helicopter needed to be prepared right away so they can head to Princess Royal Island.

As she hung up and turned to the regulars, their excited chatter filled her ears. But Baree only had one thought: she needed to find Finnian. With purpose in her step, she headed for the door. Her colleague raised his arms in query, but she did not turn back.

Every moment felt crucial as Baree made her way to the helicopter, fuelled by purpose and adrenaline. She couldn't imagine what Finnian had been through since his crash, but the thought of reuniting with him within the next 24 hours pushed her forward. This was her chance to bring him home, and nothing would stop her from finding him in that rainforest.

Baree's feet pounded the pavement as she sprinted down the street, her phone pressed to her ear. Every breath was laboured with urgency, the weight of the situation heavy on her shoulders. She dialled Grace's number, praying for her friend to pick up, but it went straight to voicemail.

"Grace, it's Baree," she spoke into the receiver, her voice steady yet tinged with trembling. "They found a beacon at an abandoned bear sanctuary on Princess Royal Island. The rescue team is ready, and there's a chance they'll find Finnian soon. I'm on my way there with Lloyd. Please keep your phone close, I'll update you. We're so close, Grace. We might finally bring him home."

Ending the call, Baree's heart raced with a mix of emotions - hope, anxiety, and a deep sense of responsibility. She knew how much this news would mean to Grace, the possibility of finding Finnian stirring every nerve in her body. But there was no time to dwell on it. Baree quickened her pace towards their destination. The journey ahead was treacherous and daunting. This time, she had to believe that they would finally bring Finnian home safe and sound.

FINNIAN

Today was the day Finnian would set off on the river, a treacherous journey that could lead him to either safety or certain death. With unbreakable focus, he began to prepare for the voyage, knowing that every moment counted in his fight for survival.

The first task was gathering the meagre food supplies he had scavenged from the abandoned log cabin. He made his way to the small pantry, forcing open the creaky door to reveal his sparse stash. Dried berries, tough strips of cured meat, a handful of nuts, and a few rusted canned goods were all he had managed to scrounge up. He carefully packed them into his pack, ensuring the weight was evenly distributed.

Inventorying his supplies with a practiced eye, Finnian noted each item with grim resolve. A small cooking pot, a water canteen, and a trusty knife were all he had to sustain him on this perilous trip. He packed them efficiently into the canoe, arranging everything within reach. The weight of his provisions caused the canoe to sit low in the water, but it remained stable.

Next, he turned his attention to the tools that could mean the difference between life and death. The rifle slung over his shoulder was a given. But he also added a small toolkit salvaged from the cabin containing wrenches, pliers, and a screwdriver. These items would prove invaluable if he needed to make any repairs along the way. He also packed a length of sturdy rope, knowing it could serve multiple purposes, such as securing the canoe or aiding in climbing.

Pausing for a moment, Finnian's gaze roamed around the desolate cabin, searching for anything he might have overlooked. His eyes fell upon a faded photograph of Jerry and Eleanor, the couple who had built this sanctuary and fiercely protected it with their lives until tragedy struck. A surge of gratitude filled Finnian's heart. He would honour their memory by surviving, by finding his way out of this unrelenting wilderness.

He tucked the cherished photograph safely into his pack as a small token of the past. And then there was the map, meticulously detailing the winding river leading to the ocean, carefully folded and placed in his jacket pocket. It was his lifeline, his guide through this treacherous terrain.

Finnian eyed the flashing beacon still pulsating its red light with unyielding strength. With all preparations complete, Finnian stepped back to survey his handiwork. The canoe was fully loaded with supplies and the gear efficiently stowed away. A mix of nerves and excitement coursed through him, anticipation of the journey forward and a fierce drive to overcome whatever challenges lay ahead.

As the sun climbed higher in the sky, casting long shadows across the forest floor, Finnian knew it was time. He took a deep breath, feeling the crisp morning air invigorate him. This was it, the beginning of the end of his harrowing ordeal.

He was ready.

Finnian stood at the edge of the river; his heart heavy with a jumble of emotions. The wooden canoe was ready, stocked with supplies for his journey away from this place. But he was unable to depart without bidding farewell to Dala, the bear who had stood by his side through all the perils and hardships of the wilderness. She watched him with her intelligent eyes, and Finnian felt a sense of sadness wash over him.

He dropped down to one knee and spoke softly to Dala, his voice trembling with emotion. "I have to go now," he said, choking back tears. "The river will take me home, but I can't bring you with me." Dala nuzzled his ear and played with his hair, reminding him of all they had been through together. "Thank you," he whispered brokenly. "For everything. Without you, I wouldn't have made it this far." He struggled to stand up, torn between wanting to stay with the bear and needing to move on. As he climbed into the canoe, he found it hard to shake off the sense of abandoning a loyal friend.

He found comfort in the familiar stability of the wooden craft below him and held onto the paddle firmly after commencing from the shore. The river's current caught hold of the canoe, propelling it forward at an alarming speed. With every stroke of the paddle, Finnian felt like he was carrying not only himself but also the weight of those who had come before him on this same journey. Together, they would fight for survival in these waters, determined to make it out alive against all odds.

Finnian's canoe bobbed gently on the river's current, the water carrying him downstream through the heart of the rainforest. He paddled steadily, his eyes scanning the horizon for any sign of the coastline.

As he rounded a bend in the river, he heard a familiar sound that made his heart ache. It was Dala, the bear, whining and howling from the riverbank. Finnian turned to see the bear pacing back and forth, its eyes wide with distress. Finnian's throat tightened as he watched the bear. It had been his protector, his companion in the wild. The bond they had formed was unbreakable, forged through countless trials and shared moments of survival. But now, as the river carried him away, Finnian felt the weight of their impending separation.

"Dala. Don't do this. Don't make this harder than it has to be!" Finnian called out, his voice cracking with emotion. The bear's whining grew more frantic; its distress penetrated the air. It tried to follow along the riverbank, but the dense underbrush and the swift current made it impossible.

Tears welled up in Finnian's eyes as he realized there was no way to bring the bear with him. The bear's place was in the forest, where it belonged.

"I'm sorry," Finnian whispered, his voice barely audible over the sound of the rushing water. "I have to go."

The bear let out a mournful roar, the sound echoing through the trees. Finnian's heart shattered at the sound, the pain of their separation cutting deep.

He watched as the bear's form grew smaller and smaller, the distance between them widening with each passing moment.

As the river carried him further downstream, Finnian clutched the wooden bear in his pocket, a small token he will keep forever, still bloodied and splintered from his fall. The tears flowed freely now, mingling with the river's spray. He knew he had to keep moving, to find his way back to safety. But the loss of the bear weighed heavily on his heart. It had been several weeks shy of two years since he first laid eyes on the bear, on Dala. The first time she had saved him.

As he drifted down the river, he whispered a silent promise to the bear he had left behind.

"I'll never forget you, Dala. I love you."

Finnian's heart ached with the loss, but he knew he had to keep moving forward. The journey ahead was uncertain, but he would face it with the strength and resilience that the bear had taught him.

The forest was eerily quiet as he glided down the calm river, its waters reflecting a serene canopy above. The bear that had taught him resilience, the lessons he had learned in this unforgiving place, they had all led him to this moment. His heart raced with anticipation as he let the current carry him towards an uncertain future. But one thing was certain: Finnian was ready to face whatever lay ahead in his journey to freedom.

The canoe sliced through the water; Finnian's mind consumed by the letter he had discovered. His predecessors, Jerry and Eleanor, had faced their own battles in the fight to protect this sanctuary, to preserve the majestic beauty of the forest. Their legacy now served as fuel for Finnian's voyage.

The river twisted and turned, revealing new landscapes and obstacles ahead. But Finnian continued to paddle with unrelenting force, his gaze fixed on the distant horizon. He didn't know what awaited him, but he knew he could not falter.

As day turned to night, Finnian found a small inlet and pulled his canoe onto shore. The forest around him teemed with nocturnal creatures, their symphony of sounds echoing through the darkness. With a small fire crackling beside him, Finnian set up camp and gazed at a photograph of Jerry and his canoe. He sighed with gratitude.

As he lay under a canopy of stars, Finnian felt a sense of peace wash over him. The river's journey was far from over, but for now, in this moment of tranquillity and solitude, he found succour. Tomorrow would bring new challenges and tests of his strength, but for now, he could rest and dream of the promise that lay ahead - the vast expanse of the ocean calling out to him like a siren's song.

BAREE

Baree and Lloyd raced through the sky above the rainforest, their helicopter slicing through the frigid air with a deafening roar. With each passing second, Baree's sharp eyes scanned the dense canopy below, her heart pounding with the desperate urgency of their mission. Every bend in the winding river was a potential clue to Finnian's whereabouts, and she couldn't afford to miss a single detail.

"Lloyd, do you see anything?" she shouted over the roaring winds, her voice laced with tension.

"Not yet," Lloyd replied, his gaze never faltering from the horizon. "We're almost at the coordinates."

The weight of their mission pressed down on them like a suffocating blanket, but Baree refused to let it crush her spirits. The forest may have been vast and unforgiving, but they had one thing on their side: the river. It was their only lifeline, a shimmering ribbon of hope leading them towards Finnian.

Just as they rounded a bend in the river, Baree's eagle eyes caught a flash of metal in the distance. "Lloyd, look!" she exclaimed, pointing towards the glimmer. "Is that another helicopter?"

Lloyd's jaw clenched as he narrowed his focus on the object in question. "Yeah," he confirmed with a determined edge in his voice. "We must be getting close."

And as if on cue, their helicopter hovered above a clearing where another chopper sat waiting for them, its rotors stirring up dust and leaves in its wake.
Adrenaline surged through Baree's veins. They were getting closer by the second.

"Lloyd, bring us lower." Her voice was steady despite the nerves coiled tightly within her stomach. "We need to coordinate with them."

With precision and skill, Lloyd descended until they were skimming just above the treetops. Baree leaned forward eagerly, her eyes scouring every inch of the riverbanks and forest floor for any sign of Finnian. The canopy may have been thick, but the river provided a clear view, each bend and turn, potentially hiding Finnian.

As they approached the clearing, Baree could make out two figures on the ground waving at them frantically, members of the search and rescue team. They had found something. Her heart raced as Lloyd gently lowered the helicopter to the ground.

Before she even stepped out, Baree was bombarded with questions from the team. "Have you seen Finnian? Did you find anything?"

Sarah, one of the search and rescue members, shook her head solemnly. "We found the cabin and the beacon, but there was no sign of him. Just a note mentioning a waterfall near the mouth of the river."

Baree's heart dropped at the mention of a waterfall. It was treacherous terrain, but if Finnian was heading there, they needed to follow.

Without hesitation, Dominic barked orders to his team. "Split up. Some of us will continue searching on foot while others scan from above."

Baree and Lloyd quickly returned to their helicopter, anticipation and fear coursing through their veins as they took off once again. The roar of the rotors drowned out any doubts or fears in Baree's mind as she focused all her energy on finding Finnian. Every beat of her heart, every breath she took, was fuelled by the strength of mind to bring him home safely.

The search continued with reinstated intensity, and Baree vowed to not rest until they found him.

FINNIAN

Finnian paddled frantically, his muscles straining against the powerful current of the river. The water surged and churned like a ferocious beast, threatening to swallow him whole. He fought against it with all his might, navigating through treacherous rapids, each one testing his limits. The force of the waves was insistent, soaking Finnian to the bone and making it difficult to keep his grip on the oars. But he refused to give up, driven by an unwavering determination to make it out alive.

As he battled the elements, hunger and thirst gnawed at him, reminding him of the dire situation he was in. Yet he pressed on, scooping up handfuls of river water to quench his thirst and nibbling on meagre rations that were all he had left from days spent navigating the churning rapids.

The forest around him seemed to close in, every rustle and cry of wildlife only adding to the sense of isolation and danger. But Finnian found solace in nature too, a deep connection to the land forged through his struggles. Just when he thought he couldn't go on any longer, a distant sound caught his attention. It was faint but unmistakable, the sound of an aircraft. With optimism, Finnian searched the sky for any sign of rescue.

Finally, he spotted it, a helicopter flying down the river. Excitement coursed through him as he waved his arms and shouted for their attention. But as the helicopter continued along the river metres in front of Finnian, desperation set in. Frantically rummaging through his pack, he pulled out a flare gun and aimed it at the sky.

The bright flare exploded into the air, but still the helicopter continued on its course. Finnian's heart sank as he watched it disappear into the distance of the trees.

BAREE

Baree's eyes darted frantically between the dense canopy below and the winding river, her heart racing with fear. The search had been gruelling; the tension mounting with every passing moment. But then, out of the corner of her eye, a sudden burst of light caught her attention. A flare, bright and unmistakable, arced through the sky.

"Look! There!" she exclaimed, striking Lloyd's shoulder in excitement and pointing towards the flare with a trembling hand. Her optimism surged, blazing like a wildfire in her chest.

Lloyd nodded, his grip on the controls steady as he expertly maneuvered the helicopter into a wide turn. The rotating blades thundered above them as they circled back towards Finnian along the river. Baree's heart pounded in anticipation, the thought of finally finding him almost too much to bear.

And then she saw it, a wooden canoe gliding along the river's surface. Tears of overwhelming joy stung her eyes, but she refused to blink and miss this long-awaited sight. "There he is," she whispered, her voice choked with emotion. "It's Finnian. He's alive!"

Finnian, battered and exhausted, lay back in the canoe with his eyes closed. After exhaling heavily, he sensed the burden of his ordeal lifting off his shoulders. He murmured to himself, a sense of peace washing over him at last. "It's finally over."

The helicopter hovered above them, a promise of rescue and safety. Baree leaned out, waving frantically as she called out to him with relief and elation in her voice. "Finnian! We're here! You're safe!"

Finnian's eyes snapped open at the sound of her voice, disbelief and joy spreading across his weary face, tears welling in his eyes. He raised a trembling arm to wave back at the helicopter, filled with a sense of triumph after days of fear and uncertainty.

Lloyd lowered the helicopter carefully, maintaining a safe distance from the rushing river. The search and rescue team on standby prepared to assist, their movements precise and efficient. Baree could hardly contain her emotions, tears streaming down her face as the reality of the moment set in.

As the helicopter settled, Baree knew that this was the end of one journey and the beginning of another. Finnian was safe, and they would bring him home. The wilderness had tested him, pushing him to his limits, but he had survived. Their unbreakable bond had led them to this moment.

The deafening roar of the helicopter, the rushing river, and the dense forest all faded into background noise as Baree focused on Finnian. They had found him. After two years, he was finally going home.

THE BEAR

The sun was just beginning to rise, casting a warm, golden light over the forest. The bear stirred from her rest. But this time, her instincts were tinged with unease. She had grown accustomed to their daily routine, yet something seemed different today.

As she followed the man through the dense underbrush, her mind raced with conflicting thoughts. On one hand, she knew it was her duty to watch over him and ensure his safety. But on the other hand, there was a growing sense of attachment and dependence between them that made her heart ache at the thought of him leaving. When he pushed his canoe into the water and began to drift away, the bear's heart was torn in two. Her loyalty and love for the man compelled her to stay by his side, even as her wild instincts urged her to let him go.

But then something inside her snapped. A primal urge took over, overpowering any logical thoughts or emotions. With an angry snarl, the bear ran after him, determined to make him stay. Her thunderous paws pounded against the ground as she raced through the forest, fuelled by a mix of desperation and fear. The river was her enemy now, carrying the man away from her grasp.

As they continued further down the river, the bear's spirit began to waver. No matter how fast she ran or how loud she roared, she understood that nothing would alter the inevitable - he was leaving. In that moment of defeat and heartache, the bear returned to the cave alone. She couldn't bring herself to follow any further or face the emptiness that awaited her back at their home.

Days turned into weeks as the bear mourned the loss of their companionship. Each day brought new struggles as she tried to reconcile the fierce love she felt for the man with the harsh reality of their separation.

The forest remained unchanged, but for the bear, everything had changed. Her purpose and identity were now in question, causing her to ponder whether she would ever find that same sense of connection and belonging again.

As she lay alone in the cave, the bear held onto the memory of him, torn between a longing for his presence and resentment for the ache he left behind. Their shared bond was a reminder that constantly brought to mind what might have occurred, a bittersweet echo of the time they faced the wild together. A whisper. A spall of the past.

But despite the pain and conflict within her, the bear knew one thing for certain - her heart would forever carry a piece of the man with it, witness to their unbreakable bond, even in the face of separation.

FINNIAN

The bustling city greeted Finnian with a cacophony of noise, honking cars, chattering crowds, the incessant hum of urban life. Upon stepping out of the taxi, the cold concrete under his feet appeared foreign and unwelcoming. His apartment, once a haven, now seemed suffocating with its walls closing in, cutting him off from the open expanse he had grown accustomed to.

Days turned into weeks, yet the relentless rhythm of city life only amplified his sense of disconnection. Finnian roamed the bustling streets, seeking comfort in familiar places, but everything seemed empty. The city's deafening roar had replaced the forest's quiet whispers. Each night, he dreamed of the wilderness, the rustling leaves, the crisp air, the solitude that had become his sanctuary.

In the midst of a joyous gathering to welcome him home, Finnian found himself lost in his thoughts about the rainforest. Despite the embraces and light conversations with

Grace, Baree and their friends and family members, he couldn't shake his thoughts of Dala from his mind.

One evening, as Finnian stood on his balcony overlooking the sprawling skyline, a pang of longing struck him deep. The city's lights, once mesmerizing, now seemed like a web of confinement. He realised he missed the stillness, the profound silence that allowed his thoughts to settle like leaves on a forest floor. The decision came like a breath of fresh air. Finnian packed his bags with a sense of purpose, each item a reminder of the life he was leaving behind. The journey back to the remote forest was a blur of anticipation and relief.

It had been two months since Finnian returned home, but his mind was far from at ease. The tranquil streets and quiet routines of his town did little to soothe the memories that haunted him. Every night, he would close his eyes and be transported back to the wilderness, the scent of pine and earth filling his senses once more. And with it came the ache in his heart for Dala, the bear he had formed an unbreakable bond with.

Unable to shake off the gnawing sense of guilt and longing, Finnian made a decision. He had to go back. He had to find Dala and make sure she was safe. With purpose in his steps, he reached out to Lloyd, his trusted helicopter pilot, and planned a trip back to Pullman's Treaty. Baree, ever supportive, refused to leave his side.

The morning, they set off was crisp and clear, the sky a flawless blue canvas stretched above them. As they climbed into the helicopter, Lloyd expertly adjusted his controls, his face serious with concentration. "You ready for this?" he asked, glancing back at Finnian and Baree.

Finnian nodded, steeling himself for what lay ahead. "I need to know she's okay," he replied.

Baree squeezed his hand, offering silent support. "We'll find her," she assured him.

The helicopter lifted off, the ground falling away as they soared over the dense canopy of the Great Bear Rainforest. The journey was filled with tense silence, each of them lost in their own thoughts. But as they neared Pullman's Treaty, Finnian felt a familiar mixture of anxiety and anticipation bubbling up inside him. The forest spread out below them like a vast green sea, mysterious and alluring.

Lloyd skilfully navigated through the trees, searching for a safe place to land. "Hold on," he called back, his voice steady and reassuring. "We're almost there."

They descended slowly; the rotors kicking up dust and leaves as they touched down near the edge of the sanctuary. Stepping out of the helicopter, peace washed over him in an instant. The familiar scent of pine and earth embraced him, and the quiet, broken only by the distant calls of wildlife, welcomed him home.

In the forest, Finnian found what the city lacked: a deep sense of belonging and healing. The solitude he had once feared became his greatest ally, and the wilderness, his sanctuary.

Finnian and Baree strode through the underbrush together, their hearts pounding with a mix of excitement and trepidation. The familiar sights and sounds of the forest surrounded Finnian, yet everything took on a new sense of purpose and urgency.

Finnian's voice held a tinge of insistence as he spoke, the worry evident in his tone. "We need to check her usual spots first."

Together, they ventured into the thick forest, calling out for Dala. The stillness that greeted them was unsettling. Finnian's heart raced with each step, his eyes darting around the trees in search of any sign of movement. Baree, experiencing the vastness of the untamed wilderness for the first time, marvelled at its raw beauty and overwhelming sense of wonder.

"It's breathtaking," she whispered in awe, taking in the towering trees and the sunlight filtering through the canopy. "I can understand why you formed such a strong bond with her."

Finnian nodded, but his mind was consumed by one thought: finding Dala. They searched every familiar spot, their voices echoing through the empty forest. But there was no trace of her. The absence of her usual sounds and movements heightened the sensation of emptiness in the forest.

Reluctantly, they climbed back into the helicopter. As Lloyd flew them to the site where Finnian had first discovered his bond with Dala - the wreckage of a plane - memories flooded back and emotions resurfaced. Finnian swallowed hard as they landed near the twisted metal and broken branches.

"We'll have to walk from here," he said firmly, his quest driving him forward.

Shouldering their backpacks, Finnian and Baree trekked through the forest, desperately searching for any sign of Dala. The silence was deafening, each unanswered call a blow to

Finnian's confidence. He expected to see her come bounding through the trees at any moment, but there was only stillness.

As they approached the area where Dala's cave lay hidden, Finnian felt a knot tighten in his stomach. He pushed forward, his heart racing with both fear and anticipation. The entrance to the cave loomed ahead, dark and ominous.

Baree watched from a distance, her heart aching for Finnian. She saw him drop to his knees just outside the cave, overcome with emotion. She noticed her breath catch in her throat as she hurried over to see what lay ahead of them.

Curled up inside the cave was Dala, her light grey fur almost blending in with the shadows. Finnian's tears streamed down his face as he crawled closer, his trembling hand reaching out to touch her. But the bear's body remained still, her spirit long gone.

"Dala," he whispered brokenly. "I'm so sorry."

Baree knelt beside him, tears streaming down her own cheeks. She looked around the small cave and noticed the scattered belongings that Dala had collected while Finnian was away. It was as if she had been holding onto pieces of him, even in his absence.

Finnian and Baree huddled at the entrance of Dala's cave, the forest around them unnervingly quiet. The air was charged with tension; every rustle of leaves magnified into a deafening roar. Suddenly, a giant shadow cast itself over them, the ground trembling beneath their feet. They turned to see a gargantuan grizzly bear looming above them, its breathing ragged and laboured. A deep, primal growl rumbled from its throat, sending shudders down Finnian's spine.

Finnian instinctively covered Baree's mouth with his hand, his voice barely a whisper as he warned her to remain still and silent. Baree nodded in understanding, her eyes wide with terror and trust. Slowly, Finnian removed his hand from her mouth and began to rise to his feet, each movement deliberate and calculated.

Standing tall and unassuming, Finnian locked eyes with the bear in an intense stare-down, a silent exchange passing between man and beast. In that moment, they were two equals, connected by an inexplicable bond. Time seemed to stand still as they gazed into each other's souls; the bear's eyes radiating wisdom and strength, while Finnian felt an overwhelming sense of peace wash over him.

Finally, the bear dropped back onto all fours and the tension dissipated. With one last look at Finnian, it lumbered off into the wilderness, seamlessly blending into its surroundings. Finnian let out a breath he didn't realise he was holding, his chest heaving with relief.

As the bear disappeared from view, Finnian caught sight of something white at the edge of the trees. His heart skipped a beat as Eleanor emerged from the shadows, flanked by two majestic cream-coloured bears. It was a surreal and poignant moment as they all turned and vanished deeper into the rainforest.

Tears streamed down Finnian's face as he stood in awe, humbled and transformed by the encounter. Baree's soft voice broke through the silence, filled with concern.

"Are you alright?" she whispered, her hand gently touching his arm.

Finnian took a moment to compose himself, his emotions raw and overwhelming. He let out a deep sigh before turning to wrap Baree in a tight embrace. "I promise, I will never let go again," he murmured into her hair, his voice filled with unshakable drive.

Baree returned the hug, her own tears mingling with Finnian's as they held onto each other. The encounter had been an intense and unforgettable connection with nature that both of them would carry with them forever.

With renewed purpose, Finnian set his sights on the journey ahead. He would honour Jerry and Eleanor's memory. He would rebuild the sanctuary and honour the legacy of Pullman's Treaty. In the name of Dala, the spirit bear of the Great Bear Rainforest.

As the helicopter took to the air for a final time, Baree slipped her hand into Finnian's as they sat beside each other. Finnian's head lulled softly against Baree's shoulder as he fell asleep. She noticed a worn notebook protruding from his pack. In one swift movement she plucked it from its pocket, manoeuvring her hand so that she wouldn't startle Finnian awake. Baree opened the notebook. Her eyes rested upon a poem:

In the heart of the forest, wild and grand,
A bond was forged between ~~beast~~ bear and man.
Through trials faced, in silence shared,
Two souls entwined; no words declared.

~~Gandalf,~~ Dala, the bear with eyes so deep, A
guardian in the nights they'd keep.
With every growl and every stare,
A silent promise, "I'm always there."

Man, lost in the wilderness vast,
Found strength in memories from the past. Through
cold and dark, through storm and strife,
He clung to hope; he clung to life.

Beside the rivers, beneath the trees,
Their spirits soared on the forest's breeze. Through
snow and rain, through sun's warm kiss,
Their bond was sealed, no love amiss.

~~In shadows danced by firelight,~~
~~Together they faced the longest night.~~
~~The bear's fierce heart, the man's strong hand,~~
~~They faced the wild as one strong band.~~

When rivers called to distant shores,
And parting paths could be ignored no more, A
tear was shed, ~~a heart~~ two hearts were torn,
Yet in their bond, new strength was born.

For in the forest, wild and grand,
The bear and man will always stand. Though
paths diverge, their spirits find,
A bond eternal, the forever kind.

The roar of the rotors a constant thrum. The lush expanse of the rainforest spread out below, a vibrant sea of green that seemed to stretch on endlessly. Baree stole a glance at Finnian; his eyes were still closed.

Her attention was drawn to the notebook she held, its pages filled with scribbles and notes. Finnian had poured his heart into those words, and Baree felt a deep connection to the emotions they contained. With gentle curiosity, her fingers tracing over the page.

As she flipped through, she came across another poem. She softly read the verses to herself, sensing the stirring of emotions within her. Unconsciously, she began to sing the poem under her breath, her voice a gentle melody that seemed to blend seamlessly with the rhythm of the helicopter. Baree's gaze remained fixed on the rainforest below. The words of the song flowed effortlessly from her lips.

Through tears and anguish, battles fiercely waged,
In the wilderness of mind, alone we've raged.
Yet from the deepest wounds, resilience grows,
In the silence of the night, hope softly glows.
Each splinter tells a story, of survival and grace,
A testament to the trials we bravely face.
Amidst the chaos, a pattern starts to form,
A mosaic of our strength, weathering the storm.

The melody filled the small cabin, a soothing balm to weary spirits. As Baree sang, Finnian felt a sense of peace wash over him as he slept. The journey had been long and arduous, but the song served as a reminder of his unbreakable spirit, and the strength he had found within himself.

The helicopter continued its flight. Baree's voice, soft yet full of emotion, blended with the hum of the rotors, creating a harmony that seemed to echo through the air.

Triumph emerges from the darkest shade,
In the cracks of our heart, courage is laid.
Every scar, a memory, of battles we recall,
Binding us together in the echoes of the spall.
Binding us together in the echoes of the spall.

In the echoes of the spall.

EPILOGUE

Trauma has a way of shaping us, moulding our edges and filling our corners with shadows we often don't recognize until we are forced to confront them. For Finnian, the wilderness was not just a physical challenge, but a confrontation with the deepest parts of himself. It was a journey through the wilds of his own soul, navigating the tangled forest of fear, regret, and promise.

The title "Echoes of the Spall" resonated deeply with Finnian's journey. Just like the spall, the fragments left behind from being broken, he carried the splinters of his past within him both physically and metaphorically. These fragments were part of his story, his identity, and his path to healing.

Dala, the bear, became a mirror to his own struggle. In her eyes, he saw reflected his own fight for survival, his own quest for meaning. She embodied the raw, untamed spirit of the forest, a creature that lived by instinct and resilience. In her presence, Finnian found a silent companion who understood the language of hardship without the need for words.

Their bond was forged in the fires of adversity; an unspoken connection that can exist between beings who share the same scars, the same battles. Dala's strength became a metaphor for Finnian's own inner fortitude. Her grace under pressure, her force to protect what was dear to her, mirrored his own journey to protect his spirit and reclaim his life.

Yet, the wilderness was also a place where Finnian confronted his deepest traumas. The pain of losing John weighed heavily on him, the grief a constant presence in the back of his mind. John had been more than a friend; he was a brother in every sense that mattered. The loss left a gaping wound in Finnian's heart, a wound that the wild seemed to understand and reflect back at him.

In the silent moments by the river, or the quiet nights under the stars, Finnian found himself grappling with the memories of John. The laughter they had shared, the adventures, and the bond that had been so abruptly severed. The forest became a place of mourning, but also a place of reflection and healing.

And then there was Patrick, the father he had always believed didn't love him. The emotional conflict of feeling unloved and abandoned by his father had gnawed at Finnian

353

for years. The wilderness, with its harsh tests and silent judgments, forced him to confront these feelings head-on. It was in the quiet companionship of Dala and the relentless trials of survival that Finnian began to understand the complexities of his father's love, and the ways in which it had always been there, even if he hadn't seen it.

Facing trauma alone is an arduous path, but Finnian's story shows that even in the darkest of forests, there are moments of light, connections that sustain us, and symbols that guide us through. His bond with Dala was a silent promise that no matter how wild the storm, there is always a way through. The bear became more than a guardian of the forest; she was a guardian of his soul, a reminder that strength lies in the heart that dares to endure.

As Finnian embraced Baree, swearing never to let go, he carried with him the lessons of the wilderness, the echoes of the spall, and the understanding that in facing his traumas, he had found not just survival, but a way to truly live. The forest had been his crucible, Dala his guide, and the journey his rebirth. In the end, the wilderness did more than test him; it transformed him, leaving behind the echoes of a life forever changed.

APPENDIX

For readers who wish to explore more of the untamed wilderness and uncover new mysteries, here's an additional chapter that delves into the unseen protector of the rainforest.

THE HUNTER

With calculated steps and controlled breaths, the hunter silently navigated the dense underbrush with a ghostly presence. The forest, a well-known friend, kept its secrets hidden for only the attentive to discover. This spot had served as the hunter's home for years, a harbour from the outside world where nature was in charge. An unspoken bond linked the hunter and the wilderness, transcending an understanding only those that bonded with the wild could truly comprehend.

Since the crash, the hunter had been quietly observing Finnian and his bear friend with keen eyes. Hidden in the shadows, always observing from a distance, the hunter had seen everything, the battle for survival, the unbreakable bond forged between man and bear. Moments of despair mingled with optimism. By acting as their hidden protector, the hunter ensured their safety without being detected.

Poachers posed a constant threat to the sanctuary. The hunter was well acquainted with their kind - greedy, ruthless, and ready to destroy everything in their path. It was expected of them to get involved and expel trespassers. The hunter acted decisively and confidently to safeguard the forest and its creatures.

From a hidden vantage point in the treetops, the hunter diligently watched the poachers, noting their actions, studying their habits. Each arrow was crafted with precision and silence in mind, making the bow a trusted ally. Each shot brought down the poachers with unfaltering precision. The hunter made sure to retrieve every arrow quickly to leave no mark on the forest.

Finnian was completely unaware of the full extent of the danger surrounding him. The hunter had ensured that. The bear had a primal connection with their guardian spirit that remained beyond their comprehension. A strong bond of reverence and understanding existed between the hunter and the forest creatures, surpassing fear.

The hunter remained in a constant state of alertness, effortlessly navigating the forest undetected. Every rustle of leaves, every snap of a twig, was analysed and understood. The forest's equilibrium hinged on a flawless execution with no margin for error.

On a moonlit night, the hunter witnessed a rare moment of peace between Finnian and his bear companion by the river, illuminated by the silver glow of the canopy. It evoked a profound sense of satisfaction and direction within the hunter. They had chosen this path to safeguard the untamed and free wilderness.

Upon Finnian's departure, the hunter experienced a mix of relief and sadness. The journey had exhausted the young man, yet it had also increased his strength and wisdom. Just like Finnian, the bear had grown - their spirit stayed strong despite all the challenges they faced.

As Finnian made his way to the river's edge, the hunter observed from afar, witnessing the beginning of his canoe journey. Finnian, departing from the shore, was silently blessed by the watchful guardian, understanding that his future would be moulded by the journey ahead.

As the canoe disappeared into the water's embrace, silence descended over the quiet forest. The hunter looked back at their familiar surroundings, surrounded by the comforting sounds of nature. There was still work to be done, threats to be guarded against. The forest needed a dedicated protector who would be ready to answer its call, regardless of the time it took.

Following that, the hunter returned to their normal routine, patrolling daily with alertness and vigilance. Despite the poachers being forced out, safety in the sanctuary was never guaranteed. Every new dawn brought with it fresh challenges and secrets to uncover.

Among the residents, a myth started spreading about a secretive protector - murmurs of an unseen guardian shielding the forest. Thus, the legend of Lerfglimu Aswegi as born.

Soft whispers drifted through the forest, tales of a spectral tracker roaming among the old trees. There were those who considered Lerfglimu Aswegi to be a supernatural entity, while others thought of it as a myth. Those aware of the truth saw the forest as their sanctuary, with the hunter as its silent guardian.

With each step taken, Lerfglimu Aswegi felt a sense of familiarity in the wilderness, finding contentment in the swaying leaves and a purpose in safeguarding the unspoiled beauty that surrounded them. The connection they shared with the forest was unbreakable, a promise to safeguard its enigmas and hidden treasures for future generations.

www.ingramcontent.com/pod-product-compliance
Lightning Source LLC
Chambersburg PA
CBHW050919030726
47503CB00007BB/2377